Radical Moves

Joe carved a wide turn on his skateboard up the tube wall, then practiced standing on his hands with the board balanced on his feet. He came out of the position by flipping down and landing with a loud whack on the skateboard.

"Way to go!" Frank and Zack yelled in unison.

Joe began skating back toward Frank and Zack when he spotted a black-clad arm stick up over the right side of the tube.

"Joe! Look out!" Frank cried.

Suddenly a leather-gloved fist hurled a large handful of nuts, bolts, and ball bearings directly in Joe's path. As the wheels of Joe's board collided with the jumble of small metal parts, the board slammed to an abrupt stop.

Joe lost his balance and, in the next moment, felt himself falling sideways—ten feet to the bottom of the ramp!

The Hardy Boys Mystery Stories

Available from MINSTREL Books

113

The

HARDY BOYS®

RADICAL
MOVES

FRANKLIN W. DIXON

A
MINSTREL®
BOOK

PUBLISHED BY POCKET BOOKS

New York   London   Toronto   Sydney   Tokyo   Singapore

This book is a work of fiction. Names, characters, places and incidents are either the product of the author's imagination or are used fictitiously. Any resemblance to actual events or locales or persons, living or dead, is entirely coincidental.

A MINSTREL PAPERBACK *ORIGINAL*

 A Minstrel Book published by
POCKET BOOKS, a division of Simon & Schuster Inc.
1230 Avenue of the Americas, New York, NY 10020

Copyright © 1992 by Simon & Schuster Inc.
Front cover illustration by Daniel Horne
Produced by Mega-Books of New York, Inc.

ISBN: 0-671-73060-6

First Minstrel Books printing April 1992

10 9 8 7 6 5 4

THE HARDY BOYS MYSTERY STORIES is a trademark of Simon & Schuster Inc.

THE HARDY BOYS, A MINSTREL BOOK, and colophon are registered trademarks of Simon & Schuster Inc.

Printed in the U.S.A.

Contents

RADICAL
MOVES

1 The Hardys Meet the Hawk

"Make way for a *serious* skateboarder, Frank!" seventeen-year-old Joe Hardy shouted.

Frank heard the roar of Joe's wheels as his brother zoomed up the curving wall of the concrete tube on his blue skateboard, which was covered with stickers. Joe made a tight turn around his brother, who was coasting easily along the flattened bottom of the tube aboard his own green and red checkered skateboard.

"And you watch where you're going, hotshot!" Frank cried out as his brother narrowly missed colliding with him.

The Hardys were inside a smooth-floored, ten-foot-wide skateboarding tubeway whose sloping walls were six feet high. The snakelike tube was

1

thirty feet long and ran in a series of S-shaped curves.

Frank, who was a year older than Joe, watched his brother carve a flashy turn high up on the tube's curving wall to slow his speed. Then Joe leaned backward, putting his weight on the back of the board. Frank heard the board's rear wheels grind and watched as Joe spun sharply at the top of the turn to reverse his direction.

The brothers had similarly athletic builds and the quick reflexes needed to make the agile skateboarding moves, but blond-haired Joe was slightly more muscular and an inch shorter than his brother. At six feet one, Frank had dark hair and eyes and wore a blue T-shirt and baggy khaki shorts. Joe wore gray shorts and a red T-shirt with his favorite rock band's logo on the front.

Grinning wide, and with an excited gleam in his blue eyes, Joe came zooming back toward his brother at top speed.

Frank crouched down and pushed off on his own board, shooting out of Joe's way right before Joe braked expertly a few inches from where Frank had just stood.

"That's radical skating for an amateur thrasher, dude," a cheerful voice called from above them.

Joe turned and looked up. A skateboarder was standing on the rim at the top of the tube. With a roar of his wheels, the boy skated down the wall and stopped a foot away from Joe. The teen was about as tall as Frank and was tanned and lanky. He wore a neon green T-shirt and matching green helmet, baggy black shorts, sneakers, gloves, and elbow and knee pads.

Joe extended his hand to the skateboarder. "Thanks, man. I'm Joe Hardy. This is my brother, Frank."

"Zack Michaels," the teen replied as he gave each of them a firm handshake.

Frank noticed Joe's eyes grow wide in surprise.

"Not Zack 'the Hawk' Michaels from L.A.?" Joe asked.

Zack grinned at Joe. "That's me. You know my work?"

Joe nodded enthusiastically. "Yeah. I saw you win the freestyle championships in L.A. on that skating show on cable. You're only the best thrasher around."

"Hey, just what is a thrasher, anyway?" Frank asked.

Zack smiled. "A thrasher is a really radical, that is, excellent, skater."

Frank stored the information. Ever since Joe had gotten seriously into skateboarding, he had been using this new lingo. And if Joe kept practicing, at the rate he was going he really would turn into a solid thrasher.

"Are you skating in the Thrashathon?" Joe asked.

Zack nodded and kicked up his board. "For sure. I wouldn't miss it."

"When's the Thrashathon?" Frank asked.

Joe groaned. "I don't believe it! You mean you've forgotten that the Bayport Thrashathon is in three days? It's Bayport's first-ever skateboarding competition. And it's going to take place right here in this park." He turned to Zack. "Did you come all the way from L.A. for it?"

Zack took off his decal-covered helmet and shook his shock of long, sandy-colored hair. "Not exactly. My dad got a job over in Clermont. We live in Bayport now."

"Are you competing on both days of the Thrashathon?" Joe asked Zack.

"Definitely," Zack replied. "I think I can make a clean sweep. I want to win the vertical ramp competition the first day, then take the downhill race the next day."

"How does the competition work?" Frank asked.

"The downhill part is an intense, totally steep two-mile race. You have to be really careful not to wipe out, and whoever crosses the finish line first wins," Zack explained. "Then there's the vertical competition, too."

"What's that like?" Frank asked.

"Skaters are scored by three teams of two judges on how well they do a series of moves on the vertical ramp," Zack said.

"The judges are usually retired pro skaters, skate shop owners, or coaches," Joe added. "I've heard the prize money is pretty good, too."

4

"First prize for each competition is two thousand bucks," Zack said with a grin. "That buys a lot of boards, let me tell you. Are you competing, Joe? It's open to amateurs and pros."

Joe shook his head. "I'm pretty good, but I'm not ready to take on the pro skaters this year."

"Me neither," Frank said, readjusting the helmet he wore. "Joe's been at it for longer than I have. But now that summer vacation is here, I thought I'd try to get the hang of it."

"That's great," Zack said, bobbing his blond head in approval. "Want to learn some really stoked-out new moves?"

"Definitely!" Joe said excitedly. "Can you show me how to do a reverse fake ollie?"

From reading Joe's skating magazines, Frank knew that an ollie was an aerial trick where the board "sticks" to the skater's feet without any help from his hands.

"All in good time, Joe," Zack said easily. "First I have to see if you can play a little follow the leader."

"We don't want to keep you from training for the Thrashathon," Frank said.

"No problem," Zack said as he casually flipped back on his board and did a wheelie. "I know who's going to be there, and it isn't anybody I haven't beaten before. I'm not worried about training."

Zack popped off his board again and flipped it over with the toe of his sneaker. He bent down to examine the trucks attached to the underside of the skateboard's wooden deck. Frank knew that the trucks were the turning mechanism of the board.

"Guess he's not worried about being overconfident, either," Frank whispered to Joe.

Joe shot Frank an annoyed look. "We're lucky to get pointers from a guy as good as the Hawk," he whispered back. "Besides, you should cut him a little slack. He's new in town."

Zack finished examining the bolts that held his wheels on the front trucks under the nose of his board. Then he flipped it over.

"Are we ready to skate?" Joe asked eagerly.

"Yeah, but not here," Zack said, glancing around at the curving tubeway they were standing in. "This tube is too narrow for us to get up any speed. Let's go find a ramp."

"There's one over there," Joe suggested, pointing to a nearby U-shaped wooden structure whose sloping walls rose nine feet from its flat bottom.

Zack wrinkled his freckled nose. "That ramp's crawling with kids. You can't have a good game of follow the leader with little squealers under your wheels."

"There's the big competition half-pipe ramp in the back of the park," Joe offered. "The walls are about twelve feet high. Maybe it hasn't been reserved." Because so many competitors were in need of practice ramps, the park officials had set up a sign-up sheet so that boarders who had entered the Thrashathon would be able to reserve ramps.

"Let's check it out," Zack said enthusiastically. "That's more my speed. Follow me!" He pushed off with his left foot and shot away like a rocket. Crouching down low on his board, he maneuvered easily around the scores of other skaters that filled the park.

Frank watched his brother and saw the determined expression on Joe's face as he tried to keep up with Zack. He knew how much his brother loved mastering a new sport and that he thrived on competition.

As Frank followed Joe and Zack, he glanced around Bayport's new outdoor skating park. It was on a square-shaped lot surrounded by a redbrick wall. Ramps of varying heights had been set up along the wall. Smaller half-pipe ramps, miniramps, and other skating areas were laid out in the center of the park. Across the park, opposite the redbrick wall, was a brightly colored snack bar, a skateboard repair shop, and the park office.

Though the park had only been open a month, it was already packed with skaters of all ages, and the mood inside its walls was electric. The air was filled with happy, shouted conversations and laughter punctuated by rap and heavy metal music blaring from loudspeakers. The speakers were mounted on tall pillars painted in vivid Day-Glo orange and green. The pillars had been plastered over with decals from various skateboarding companies and rock bands.

The skaters' clothes added to the circuslike atmosphere in the park. Most of them wore the same bright neon colors on their helmets, clothes, and safety pads that were used to decorate the park.

Every skater Frank passed wore a hard plastic helmet with a chin strap, along with gloves and elbow and knee pads. Frank had only been skateboarding for a short time, but he already knew how easy it was to get hurt. So he hadn't minded the wait to enter the park while the security staff checked out each skater's safety gear. The staff had refused admittance to several skaters who weren't wearing helmets.

"Hey, Joe, wait up," Frank called.

But Joe was too far ahead to hear him. Cutting a move through the long line of kids waiting to buy sodas and burgers at the snack bar, Frank skated quickly over the park's smooth concrete walkways. As he rounded a big tree, he saw the competition ramp. Joe and Zack were the only skaters there.

"Joe, can you handle this ramp? It looks a bit steep," Frank commented as he skated up alongside his brother.

"What do you think I am—a geek?" Joe responded. "This ramp is a piece of cake."

Frank looked over at the ramp again. It was U-shaped and had curving twelve-foot-high electric blue walls that were set thirty feet apart. The ramp's smooth surface was made from sheets of painted plywood that had been nailed to the frame. The whole structure was supported by a framework of steel pipes with two-by-fours at either end. There were also two-foot-wide walkways along the top for the skaters to stand on. The ramp had been built right next to the nine-foot-high redbrick wall that ran around the perimeter of the park.

Even though Joe was willing to ride the ramp, Frank didn't want to give it a try. Generally more cautious and methodical than his impulsive younger brother, Frank knew that these qualities helped make him a good detective. Joe was a talented detective, too, but he often relied on flashes of inspiration during a case. Despite the differences in their personalities, Frank and Joe were a great detective team.

"Watch this!" Frank heard Zack call out.

Zack streaked up the wall toward the rounded steel edge at the very top—the "coping." Then he sailed up into the air past the coping, crouching low over his board with his feet planted sideways on either end. Zack seemed to hang in midair for a second. Before he could fly off the ramp, he shifted his weight toward the front end of the board, hit the ramp, and began his descent. It was a classic "pop off," one Frank had read about in the skating magazines and even seen on TV. But Zack made it seem so easy. Frank could see why his nickname was "Hawk."

Zack hit the bottom of the slope and popped his board into a back wheelie, spinning around in rapid circles with the board's nose in the air.

"Okay, Joe, your turn," Zack said slyly, his green eyes sparkling.

Joe ran a gloved hand through his hair and chuckled. "I don't think I can follow that trick."

"It's easier than it looks," Zack told him. "The secret is getting up enough speed as you come up to the curve of the ramp. You've got to be really flying when you come to the coping. The best pop offs happen with a lot of speed. But don't overdo it, or you'll fly off instead of pop off!"

Joe laughed. "I see what you're driving at, but how do you get so much speed?"

"Let me show you," Zack said to Joe. "Watch closely."

Zack climbed back up to the walkway and positioned himself at the edge of the ramp. He pushed off on his board, dropping in on the curving ramp wall. He raced into the bottom of the ramp at full speed, then came into the opposite curve of the ramp. He crouched low over his board, leaning forward as he zoomed up toward the coping at the top of the opposite wall. He held his arms out for balance with his palms facing down and his feet wide apart.

Frank watched Zack approach the top of the ramp to execute his midair trick. The thrasher was really flying. This move was even better than the last one he did.

"This guy's great!" Frank called to his brother.

Frank held his breath as Zack started to pop off from the coping. But right at that moment, Frank

10

spotted a black-clad arm suddenly shoot out from the walkway at the top of the ramp.

"Zack, watch out!" Frank cried.

But it was too late. Before Zack had time to react, the hand grabbed Zack's board—right out from under him!

2 Dirty Tricks

"Zack!" Joe shouted, hearing his brother's cries and realizing what was happening. "He's going to fall!" Joe yelled as he saw Zack's fingers grab at the ramp coping.

"Hold on!" Frank cried out to Zack.

Joe watched in horror as the metal coping gave way under Zack's grip. The thrasher let out a howl of pain as he fell from the coping, sliding down the ramp's steep face. Zack landed at the bottom of the ramp with a solid thump.

Joe and Frank ran to help. Before he reached Zack, Joe looked up at the narrow walkway. The guy who had grabbed Zack's board was lying on his stomach on the walkway, trying to prevent the board from falling over the edge of the ramp. The culprit was dressed in black and wore a motorcycle helmet with a black face visor.

"You take care of Zack," Joe shouted to his brother. "I'm going to nab that guy!"

The helmeted thief was pulling the board up over the coping, but at the last minute Zack's board slipped from his grasp and rattled down the ramp. It landed right next to Zack.

Joe raced for the board and watched as Zack's assailant got to his feet and started to scramble down a ladder that was bolted to the support beams.

"Oh, no, you don't," Joe yelled as he jumped off the ramp and ran over to the ladder. He quickly climbed up the ladder toward the figure in black, who then decided not to take the ladder down. As soon as Joe reached the top of the ladder, the person jumped from the ramp to the nearby brick wall.

Joe tried to grab him, but Zack's assailant spotted him, turned and gave the younger Hardy a push that sent Joe flying off the skate ramp.

Joe felt himself begin to fall backward toward the steep wall of the ramp. Lurching toward the right, he reached for the edge of the ramp but only got a fistful of air. He landed on his right side and began rolling down the ramp sideways. Seconds later, he hit the bottom of the ramp. Joe lay there for a moment, stunned and dizzy, trying to get his breath back.

"Joe, are you okay?" Frank asked anxiously, leaning over his brother.

"Yeah, I'm fine," Joe said, getting to his feet. "I just want to catch that joker."

"There he is!" Frank shouted, pointing to the assailant as he ran away on the top of the brick wall. Joe saw that the black-clad figure carried a battered black skateboard in his right hand. To Joe's astonishment, the helmeted man mounted his board and rode off along the level top of the wall.

"I'm not going to lose him this time," Joe called to his brother.

While Frank hurried back to where Zack lay on the ramp's floor, Joe dashed around to one end of the ramp and climbed back up the ladder. He got to the top just in time to see the mystery skater soar off the brick wall and land with a screech of his wheels on the park pavement. The skater recovered quickly and took off at a sizzling pace toward the turnstiles at the park's entrance, all the way on the other side of the park.

"Somebody stop that guy in black!" Joe shouted through cupped hands. But he knew his words would be lost in the noise of rock music and the whizzing sound of skateboard wheels on concrete.

Joe watched in frustration as the skater zipped around a corner of the park's skateboard rental and repair shop and darted out of sight. Joe climbed back down the ladder, realizing there was no point in continuing to chase the skater.

"He got away clean," Joe told his brother and Zack once he had joined them at a bench next to the competition ramp. Zack's face was white, and there was an ugly bruise coming up on his right cheekbone.

"How are you feeling?" Joe asked Zack.

"I've been better," Zack wheezed.

"Don't try to talk," Frank said. "Take it easy until your wind comes back." Turning to Joe, Frank asked, "Did you get a good look at the guy?"

Joe shook his head. "All I can tell you is that he was wearing a black motorcycle helmet with a dark visor, and had on black gloves, pads, shirt, and pants. And that he was at least as tall as me. That's all I saw. He was a good skater, too. Not many guys could've ridden along the top of that wall like he did without wiping out."

Joe reached out a hand and helped Zack to his feet. "Glad you didn't get creamed too bad, Zack."

"Me, too," Zack replied. He touched the bruise on his cheek and sighed. "I thought leaving L.A. would break the jinx, but it seems to have followed me to Bayport."

Joe glanced at Zack, then shot his brother a questioning look. Frank picked up on Zack's words in an instant. "What 'jinx' is that?" he asked. "What happened in L.A.?"

Joe watched Zack hesitate for a moment. Finally, he said, "Twice before I left L.A. I got jumped on the street by a bunch of guys I didn't know." He

15

looked at the Hardys, a frightened expression on his face. "It was pretty scary. Those guys really worked me over. They tried to take my new board, but I managed to hang on to it."

"Was one of the guys who jumped you dressed like the skater who attacked you today?" Joe asked.

Before Zack could answer, Frank said, "Did anyone back in L.A. have a grudge against you?"

Zack frowned. "You guys ask a lot of questions. What are you, cops?"

"Not exactly," Frank said with a smile. "Actually, Joe and I are detectives."

Wearing an uncertain expression, Zack looked back and forth between the Hardys as if he thought they were pulling his leg.

"No way," said the thrasher.

Joe grinned. "Yes way," he said.

"So, what do you guys investigate?" Zack asked cautiously.

"Anything that doesn't add up," Frank told him. "I can't put my finger on it yet, but something tells me there's more to these attacks on you than just coincidence. I mean, doesn't it seem strange that you've been attacked in Bayport, too?"

"Tell you what," Joe began. "You help us with our skating, and we'll help you with your problem."

"Uh, I don't know," Zack said hesitantly.

"Relax," Joe said, smiling. "Frank and I are serious. Being detectives runs in our family. Our dad, Fenton Hardy, is a detective, too."

Zack looked at Frank and Joe for a moment, biting his lip thoughtfully. "Okay, you've got a deal," he said finally.

"Great!" Frank shouted. Joe could tell his brother was excited to be back on a case.

"Is there anybody in Bayport who would want to torpedo you?" Frank asked.

Zack shrugged. "Beats me, Frank. I've only been here about two weeks, not long enough to make many friends, let alone enemies." He glanced at his watch, and a startled expression came over his face. "Yikes. It's quarter to one already," he said. "I told my mom I'd be home by noon." He got up from the bench, threw down his skateboard, and stepped onto it.

"Hey, what about our skating lessons?" Joe called after Zack as he zipped away.

"I'll see you two here, same ramp, at nine tomorrow morning," Zack shouted over his shoulder. Then he began to swiftly weave in and out of the crowds of skaters, and Joe lost sight of him.

"He's some skater," Joe said with more than a hint of admiration.

"He also seems to be in some trouble," Frank added. "I just hope we can help him."

The next morning Joe was so eager to join Zack at the skateboarding park that he barely let Frank grab a piece of toast on the way out of the house. When they reached the park, they paid their

17

admission, passed through the turnstiles, and skated toward the U-shaped ramp on the opposite side of the park. Even though the Thrashathon was still two days away, the park was alive with activity.

"Any sign of Zack?" Frank asked Joe as they scanned the crowds of brightly dressed skaters.

"No, but check out that TV crew over there," Joe said, pointing toward a cameraman and a sound man carrying a big tape recorder and a long sound boom. Joe noticed that the men accompanied a red-haired woman reporter, who was interviewing a skater. She was dressed in white shorts and a neon orange T-shirt with the words "National Thrasher" printed across the front.

"That reporter is Maggie Barnes, one of the hosts of the 'National Thrasher' show on cable," Joe told his brother. "She also writes for *Orb*, the skateboarding magazine."

While Frank watched the pretty, blue-eyed reporter, Joe kept his eyes peeled on the front gate for some sign of Zack. Finally, he saw a green and black blur as Zack suddenly popped into view.

Stopping his board several feet before he got to the turnstiles, Zack put one foot on the board and sent it shooting under the turnstiles. He quickly vaulted over the turnstiles and landed squarely on his board while it was still rolling. Zack whizzed through the crowd, glided to a perfect stop, then spun three times on his back wheels to end up next to the Hardys.

"Hi, guys. Am I late?" Zack asked.

"Only a few minutes," Frank replied. "But it was worth it to see you do that turnstile trick."

"Maggie Barnes from 'National Thrasher' is here," Joe told him. "Do you know her?"

"I sure do," Zack said, a huge grin spreading across his face. "Where is she?"

Before Joe could point Maggie out, Zack jumped up on the wide base that supported one of the loudspeaker pillars. He waved both arms overhead and shouted, "Maggie! Hey, Maggie! Over here!"

Joe saw Maggie Barnes stop her interview in midquestion wearing an expression of annoyance. When she spotted Zack, her face lit up in a grin as broad as his. "Zack—you maniac! I'll talk to you later! I'm working!" she shouted at him.

"Great!" Zack exclaimed, then hopped down to rejoin the Hardys.

"If the press is here, does that mean all the skaters have arrived?" Frank asked.

"Yeah, most of them are here already," Zack replied. "I'll give you the who's who." He scanned the crowd, shading his eyes with a gloved hand.

"Look over by the snack bar, guys," Zack told them. "See those four skaters wearing black and white zebra-striped shirts and helmets? That's the team Zebra Skateboards is sponsoring."

"How many people are usually on a team?" Frank asked.

"It depends on how many skaters a company can afford to sponsor," Zack said. "Anywhere from one to six people."

19

Joe saw Zack shift his gaze to the skate shop next to the round snack bar.

"See the tall, dark-haired guy with the yellow bandanna? He's standing with the blond woman in black jeans and the Howling Wheels T-shirt."

"Yeah," Joe answered, adding, "Isn't that guy 'Rocket Ricardo' Torres?"

Joe recognized Torres from his picture in the skateboarding magazines. He was a muscular, deeply tanned teenager, about Frank's height. Torres was dressed in a yellow T-shirt bearing the Howling Wheels logo: a flaming skateboard wheel rolling under the words Howling Wheels. Torres's helmet, which he held by its chin strap, was black with yellow trim. His gloves, pads, and shorts were also black with yellow trim.

Joe glanced over at Torres's companion. She was small and thin. Her short hair was bleached a pale blond color and stuck out in punky spikes, giving her a cool, tough look.

"Rick Torres is my ex-best friend and teammate," Zack said, the smile leaving his face.

"Why 'ex-friend'?" Joe asked.

"Ah, it's a long, boring story," Zack said slowly. "Basically the punch line is that Rocket hates my guts now. The woman is Barb Myers, my old sponsor. She owns the Howling Wheels. She hates my guts even worse than Rick does."

Joe stored the information away, thinking about the guy who'd made Zack wipe out the day before.

20

"What exactly do sponsors do for skaters?" Frank asked Zack.

"When an amateur skater starts winning competitions, one of the skateboarding companies usually offers to sponsor him," Zack explained. "Sponsors give you their skateboards and clothes and pay you to travel around to skate shops and hype their stuff."

"It's a good deal," Joe commented. "Just what happened between you and Barb Myers?"

Zack made a face and shrugged. "I guess she wasn't too happy after I quit skating for the Howling Wheels team," he said. "She accused me of being a traitor because I skated against the Howling Wheels guys in a couple of competitions."

Joe was about to ask more questions when he heard a soft voice say, "Excuse me." He turned his head and saw Maggie Barnes edge past him. The reporter stepped up to Zack and gave him a hug.

"It's good to see you, Zack," Maggie said warmly. "When did you hit town?"

"I've been in Bayport two weeks," Zack answered. "I live here now."

"Oh, so this is where you moved," Maggie said with interest. "I lost track of you for a while."

Zack dropped his eyes and studied the pavement between the scuffed toes of his sneakers. "I skated without a sponsor in a few competitions. Then I had to quit skating for a couple weeks so I could help my folks pack up our house." He motioned toward the

21

Hardys. "But enough about me. I want you to meet two of the raddest guys in Bayport—Joe and Frank Hardy."

"Hi, I'm Maggie Barnes," she said, shaking hands with Frank and Joe.

The loudspeaker they were standing under suddenly began blasting out rap music at an earsplitting volume.

"It's kind of loud here," Maggie shouted to Zack and the Hardys. "Let's find someplace more quiet so we can talk."

"Follow me," Joe shouted back, moving toward the competition ramp Zack had used yesterday.

"So, Zack, what are you doing now?" Maggie began as they headed for the ramp.

As Zack opened his mouth to answer, Joe heard the whizzing sound of a skateboard traveling at high speed.

He looked over at the ramp and saw "Rocket Rick" Torres skating down its wall. Torres hit the curve of the ramp at top speed and shot into the air. He was going so fast that his path took him right off the ramp.

Joe looked on, speechless, as he realized what Torres was up to. The Rocket was flying, top speed, aimed like a human arrow straight at Maggie and Zack!

3 Rocket Rick

"Maggie! Zack!" Frank cried. "Get down!"

The thrasher and the reporter turned around in a flash. Frank saw a look of fear in Maggie's eyes when she realized what was happening.

Frank lunged forward, grabbed Maggie's arm, and pulled her down onto the pavement. She shrieked in surprise as Frank's tackle landed them both in a rolling tumble. Out of the corner of his eye, Frank saw Joe dive for Zack and knock him out of Torres's path. Frank pushed himself and Maggie flat onto the pavement as Torres flew over them, the board's wheels coming within inches of their heads.

"What on earth?" the reporter cried, her blue eyes wide with fear. "What just happened?"

Frank heard peals of laughter and turned to see

Barb Myers, the owner of Howling Wheels, doubled over in amusement.

"Are you okay?" Frank asked with concern as he helped Maggie Barnes to her feet. "I'm sorry I had to knock you down."

Maggie stood up and rubbed her elbow. "I'm fine. Just a little bruised, that's all," she said. "You don't owe me an apology, Torres does!"

"Hey, what happened?" Frank heard somebody cry. He looked up to see Maggie's tall, skinny cameraman put down his camera and come running toward them.

"I'm all right, Bob," Maggie replied. "Just help me find someplace to sit down."

Frank watched her walk away, leaning heavily on Bob's arm. Then he turned and headed over to where Joe was helping Zack to his feet.

"Everybody okay?" Frank asked.

"I'm not hurt, just steamed!" Joe said angrily.

"If Torres thinks he can make a chump out of me in front of everybody, he's got another think coming," Zack said between clenched teeth.

He stalked off toward Rick, who was now standing with Barb Myers. Rick looked over at Zack and said something to Barb that Frank couldn't hear. Barb started to laugh again.

"Come on, Joe," Frank said. "We'd better make sure Zack doesn't get into trouble."

"I'd rather help him pay back Torres for nearly hitting us," Joe said angrily. He started toward the dark-haired skater.

"Chill out, Joe," Frank said quietly.

His brother stopped short and nodded. "Okay, okay," Joe muttered. "I'll help keep the peace. But it won't be easy."

Frank looked over at Zack and saw him shove Rick hard in the shoulder. Breaking into a run, the Hardys arrived just in time to stop a full-blown fight. Frank grabbed Zack by both elbows, while Joe stepped in front of Rick.

"Hey, just cool it, pal," Joe said to Torres. "You've caused enough trouble today."

"I'm no pal of yours," Torres said as he tried to step around Joe. "And I'm no pal of his, either."

"Hey, guys, it was just a little game," Barb Myers laughed in a husky voice. "Nothing Zack can't handle."

"Let me at him!" Zack yelled as he struggled against Frank's firm grip.

"Calm down, Zack," Frank said quietly in his ear. "We're on your side, remember?" He felt Zack relax a bit and heard him take a deep breath. Frank let go of his elbows, then put his arm around Zack's shoulders. "Show them they can't get to you."

Barb Myers's red-lipsticked mouth widened into a nasty grin. "Boy, were you scared, Zack Michaels. Some thrasher you are. Looks like you left all your guts back in L.A." Turning on her heel, she called over her shoulder to Rick, "Come on, Rocket, let's blow this scene."

Torres backed off from Joe and gave Zack a dirty

25

look. "This isn't the end of it, Zack. I'm going to get even with you for what you did to me!" Then he ran off after Barb.

"Why does Torres want to get even with you?" Joe asked.

"I guess he's just ticked off because I beat the Howling Wheels team in a big competition in L.A.," Zack replied slowly. Then he abruptly changed the subject. "Do you guys want to meet some of the other skaters and sponsors?"

Joe started to ask Zack a question about Rick, but Frank frowned at him and shook his head slightly. Zack obviously didn't want to talk about his former buddy right now.

"That would be great," Frank said, noticing the look of relief on Zack's face as the skater glanced around the park. Zack motioned to the Hardys to follow him over to one of the small covered patios that dotted the park. "There's Chris Hall, the president of Scorpion Boards, in Boston," Zack told Frank and Joe. "I'll introduce you to him."

When they reached the patio, Zack stepped up to a man of average height with light brown hair and blue eyes that twinkled in a round, freckled face.

"How are you doing, Chris?" Zack said, smiling at the man.

"Zack! Good to see you!" Chris Hall replied warmly.

After shaking hands with Hall, Zack said, "Chris,

I want you to meet Frank and Joe Hardy. They're friends who are helping me out with a little problem."

Hall flashed a big smile, then gave Frank and Joe a firm handshake.

"Nice to meet you guys," Hall said. "Any friends of Zack are friends of mine."

Standing just behind Hall in the shade, Frank noticed a skateboarder dressed in a blue and black skating outfit. With an intense expression, he glared at Zack.

"Well, well, if it isn't Zack 'the Hawk,'" the tall, black-haired skater said in a deep voice. "Where have you been hiding?"

Frank saw anger suddenly replace the twinkle in Hall's eyes.

"Put a lid on it, Danny!" Hall snapped. Then he turned to Zack. "Sorry, kid. Danny's just a little edgy today. You know how it is with the Thrashathon coming up in only two days."

"It's cool," Zack said in a low voice. Then he looked Danny straight in the eye. "Ready to get beaten in the Thrashathon, Hayashi?"

"Yeah, right. Dream on, you wimp," the muscular skater retorted. "When I beat you on Saturday, it'll be the most righteous day of my life."

Hall grabbed Danny Hayashi by the elbow and began to lead him away. "We should talk later, Zack," he called over his shoulder. "Maybe I can buy you dinner."

27

"That'd be great, Chris," Zack replied. Then, turning to Frank, he added, "Yuck. Danny Hayashi leaves a bad taste in my mouth."

"Hayashi seems to have some kind of grudge against you, just like Torres and Myers," Joe pointed out. "You know, for someone who seems like a nice guy, you have a lot of enemies."

"Hayashi's a poor loser," Zack said in a sullen tone. "He's just jealous because he's never beaten me in a competition. He's a big baby."

"Is that all there is to it?" Frank asked. "That doesn't really explain Rick's little stunt just now. Or why Barb was so happy about it."

"No, I guess it doesn't." Zack paused for a moment, then quickly changed the subject. "Look, guys, I want to go home and work on my board. I notice the trucks are loose. Wanna come with me? I can show you my workshop."

"Why don't we stop by later this afternoon?" Frank suggested. "Joe and I can stick around, maybe get in another skating session." He gave Joe a look that said he wanted to talk—and not around Zack Michaels. The skater had been a little too hesitant to answer questions about Rick and Danny. And Rick and Barb's behavior toward Zack had been hostile, as if there were more going on between them than competition or letting go of a sponsor.

Joe picked up on Frank's cue. "Give us your address, and we'll catch up with you later," he said to Zack.

"Okay," Zack said with a shrug. "I live at Three-three-one-nine Birch Street. Come by whenever." He put one foot up on his board and pushed off with the other foot. Soon he vanished into the crowds of skateboarders that filled the park.

As soon as Zack left, Joe turned to his brother and said, "Okay, Frank. I recognize that look on your face. What gives?"

Frank thought for a moment. "Zack's obviously hiding something about his relationship with Torres. And maybe Hayashi, too," he said, rubbing his chin thoughtfully. "It's strange the way he avoids our questions. And he's pretty hotheaded, too. Maybe he got himself into some kind of trouble he doesn't want to tell us about. That could be why someone is after him."

"It's a thought," Joe said, stepping out of the way of a passing skateboarder. "I like Zack, but I have to admit he's not helping us out a lot. All his explanations have to do with how he's so great and how everyone's jealous of him. That doesn't give us much to go on, does it?"

Frank shook his head. "Nope. But it's going to be impossible to learn anything from Torres or Hayashi now that they know we're Zack's friends," he pointed out.

Then Frank had a sudden thought. "Hey. Why don't we talk to Maggie Barnes?" he suggested. "She's a friend of Zack. And she must know Torres and Hayashi if she covers the skateboarding scene."

"Great idea." Joe stepped on his board and said, "Follow me. And watch out for flying boarders."

Joe soon spotted Maggie Barnes under one of the covered patios. The reporter and her video crew had taken it over as a temporary headquarters. Maggie sat in a canvas director's chair surrounded by metal equipment boxes and stacks of video monitors. She was studying some papers on a clipboard, her brow wrinkled in thought. She looked up and smiled as the Hardys walked over to her.

"How are you feeling?" Joe asked the reporter.

"Better," she replied with a grin. "Where's Zack?"

"He went home to work on his board," Frank told her. "Actually, we came to ask you a few questions about him."

"Sit down," Maggie said, pointing to the equipment box next to her chair. "What do you want to know?"

"How did Zack and Rick Torres become enemies?" Frank asked bluntly as he sat down next to Joe.

"I'm not sure," Maggie answered honestly. "Zack never told me. He and Rick used to be really tight."

"You and Zack are friends," Joe put in. "Didn't he talk to you about it?"

Maggie shook her head. "Zack was acting weird

before he left L.A. He didn't even call me to say goodbye."

"Was there any kind of trouble between them before Zack left L.A.?" Frank prodded.

"No . . ." Maggie began, then stopped as if she suddenly remembered something. "You know, Rick and Zack used to work for the same bike shop. I heard Rick got fired right after Zack left town."

"You think there's a connection?" Joe asked quickly.

"Maybe," Maggie answered. "They both worked part-time at the Alpine Mountain Bikes factory in L.A."

"I thought Zack worked for the Howling Wheels skating team," Frank said in a puzzled tone.

"He skated for the Howling Wheels team, but the company just supplied him with skateboards and gear. It's a small company. Barb Myers can't afford to pay her team anything but travel money. That's why Zack and Rick had to have jobs."

"Do you have any idea why Danny Hayashi hates Zack?" Frank asked.

"Danny hates most people, not just Zack," Maggie said. "He's a mean guy." Maggie then looked from Frank to Joe. "What's going on?" she asked, concerned. "Is Zack in trouble?"

"He might be," Frank said. He told Maggie what had happened to Zack on the ramp the day before.

31

"That could have been just a prank, or some other skater trying to psych out Zack before a big meet," Maggie said when Frank had finished. "Stuff like that happens sometimes."

"We hope it was just a prank," Joe told her.

"Well, thanks for the info, Maggie," Frank said as he stood up.

"Any time," Maggie replied. "If he's really in trouble, let me know if there's anything I can do to help."

"We will," Frank promised.

"What's our next move?" Joe asked as they stepped away from the patio.

"We look for a phone," Frank replied. "I want to call Zack's old company and ask a few questions about him."

While Joe went off to buy some chili dogs and sodas for lunch, Frank found a bank of pay phones next to the snack bar. He used his phone credit card to call Los Angeles. After getting the number from the operator, Frank called the Alpine Mountain Bikes factory.

A switchboard operator put Frank's call through to the manager.

"Hello, this is Fred Travers," a gruff voice answered. "What can I do for you?"

"This is, uh, Ted Smith," Frank said in his most businesslike voice. "I run a bike shop in Bayport. There's a job application here from a young man who used to work for your company."

32

"Who's that?" Travers asked.

"Zack Michaels."

There was a moment of silence, then an explosion of anger from the factory manager.

"You'd be crazy to hire him!" Travers shouted. "Zack Michaels is nothing but a low-down thief!"

4 The Mystery Skater Strikes Again

Frank felt a combination of excitement and shock. If Zack was a thief, it would explain why he acted so suspiciously. But Frank was surprised to hear this about Zack. "Michaels was fired for stealing?" he asked the manager in a serious tone. "He didn't tell me about that."

"He wouldn't have," Travers said hotly. "And no, he wasn't fired. He quit. I only discovered that something was missing a few weeks later."

"You have proof that Zack Michaels was the thief?" Frank asked.

"Only a handful of people had access to the area where the theft occurred. Zack was one of them, and after I checked out the other employees, I decided that he was the most likely suspect."

Travers paused. "I had to fire another employee, a friend of Zack's who had access to the same area. Even though he denied any involvement, I felt he was lying. I was sure they both planned the theft."

"Were the police called in?"

"No," Travers said after a few moments. "I didn't call the police. The company didn't want any publicity, and I didn't have enough evidence to arrest Michaels. But I'm sure he was the thief."

"Can you tell me what was stolen?" Frank asked, trying to keep the excitement from his voice.

There was a long pause at the other end of the line before Travers answered cautiously, "I'm afraid I can't tell you, Mr. Smith. That's privileged information."

"Some kind of trade secret?" Frank asked, trying to sound as though he was making a joke.

"Something like that," Travers replied, adding, "Look, I've got some other calls to make—"

"I've just got one more question," Frank quickly interrupted. "Was Zack's friend at your company named Ricardo Torres?"

From the tone of Travers's voice, Frank knew his question had surprised the manager. "How do you know that?" Travers sputtered.

"Uh, because Zack Michaels also used Torres for a reference," Frank answered quickly. "He said they used to work together at Alpine Bikes."

"Then Zack's not just a thief, he's an idiot, too," Travers said disgustedly. "After I fired Torres, he swore he'd get even with Zack."

35

"Well, thanks for your time, Mr. Travers," Frank told him. "After what you've told me, I certainly won't hire Zack Michaels."

"Good!" Travers snapped. "That little weasel is nothing but trouble."

Frank hung up the phone and gave a low whistle. "Well, what do you know about that," he commented.

"About what?" Joe stood behind Frank, a box of chili dogs and two sodas in his hands. "From the look on your face, I'd say you just learned something very interesting," Joe said as Frank took a chili dog and soda from the box.

"Good guess," Frank replied. He scanned the area and spotted an empty patio nearby. "Let's go over there. I can fill you in while we're eating."

Balancing their sodas and chili dogs in one hand, and their skateboards in another, the Hardys made their way to an empty table.

"Okay, what did you find out?" Joe asked as he sat down.

Frank took a bite of his chili dog before answering. "After Zack quit his job at Alpine, the manager discovered that something was stolen from the area where Zack worked."

"Like what?" Joe asked curiously.

"The guy wouldn't say."

Joe looked confused. "I don't get it. What does Zack being accused of stealing have to do with the guy who made him wipe out?" he asked.

36

Frank swallowed and said, "The manager told me that Rick Torres got fired because he was suspected of helping Zack steal from the company. And Torres swore he'd get even with Zack."

"That would explain why Torres and Zack are enemies now," Joe said.

"It also puts Rick Torres at the top of our suspect list as the mystery skater," Frank said. "He may be trying to get revenge on Zack by making sure he doesn't skate in the Thrashathon."

"Let's head to Zack's house now," Joe suggested, gulping the last of his soda. "Zack Michaels has some explaining to do."

Fifteen minutes later, Joe was pulling the Hardys' van into Zack's driveway. The house was in a residential neighborhood only a few blocks from Bayport's huge new shopping mall. It was a white two-story house with a separate garage and a large yard surrounded by a six-foot-high wooden fence. A mud-spotted dirt bike was parked on the driveway in front of the two-car garage. Most of the other houses on the street looked like Zack's. The one across from Zack's house was empty and had a For Sale sign in the front yard.

The Hardys mounted the steps to the Michaelses' front door. Frank rang the doorbell several times, but there was no answer.

"Maybe Zack's in the garage," Joe suggested. They followed the brick walk that ran between the

37

house and the garage. Joe rapped sharply on the garage's side door.

"Who is it?" Zack's voice called from inside.

"It's Frank and Joe Hardy," Joe called through the door.

Zack pulled the door open and motioned them inside. "Welcome to the Hawk's Lair," he said with a grin.

"This is a great setup you've got here," Joe said as he looked admiringly around the garage that Zack had converted into a skateboard workshop. A long table covered with tools, extra wheels, and skateboard trucks stood against the back wall. An old sofa and several chairs were arranged in the center of the room. A battered wall unit with a stereo and TV blocked off the garage's doors. Skateboarding magazines littered the floor.

"Yeah, it was really cool of my parents to let me take over the garage," Zack said, pulling open the door of a small fridge. He tossed cans of cold soda to Frank and Joe.

"Do you build your own boards here?" Joe asked as he popped open his can.

"Uh-huh. I started making my own boards back in L.A. At first I was just upgrading wheels and stuff on my old boards," Zack replied as he settled into the sofa. "Now I'm starting to design from scratch."

"Your custom board is hot, Zack. Have you tried selling that design to one of the skateboard companies?" Joe asked.

"Actually, one of them *is* interested in my

38

board," Zack said slowly. "But I really can't talk about the deal until it's finalized."

Frank cleared his throat and got right to the point. "We didn't just come here to see your workshop or talk about boards, Zack."

"Oh, yeah? What do you want to talk about?" Zack asked. Joe noticed that he was nervously fidgeting with his soda can.

"Alpine Bikes and Rick Torres," Frank said bluntly.

Zack looked down at the can in his hand. "I already told you about Torres," Zack muttered.

"Look, we know Rick got fired from Alpine Bikes," Frank told him. "I spoke to the manager. He claimed you stole something from his factory."

Zack looked up, his face red with anger. "You had no right to do that!" he said hotly. "My past is none of your business!"

"Maybe not," Joe admitted. "But you do want us to find out who the mystery skater is, don't you? Maybe it's someone out for revenge—like Rocket Rick Torres."

The expression of anger left Zack's face, and he slumped against the cushions of the sofa. "I don't know," he said with a sigh. "It could be Rocket. I mean, he's mad enough to try something like that, but I just don't know."

"Maybe if you told us more about what happened at Alpine Bikes, we could help you," Frank said quietly.

"Okay," Zack said reluctantly. "But do you guys

mind if we do it out by the pool? It's easier for me to talk when I'm riding my board."

"Sure," Joe replied.

"Great," Zack said, looking relieved. He stood up and grabbed his board from the workbench. "My parents haven't had the pool filled yet, so they're letting me skate in it for now."

Zack led the Hardys out of the workshop and closed the door behind him. Then the three teens headed down the brick path to the backyard. Zack had his board tucked under one arm. When they got to the pool area, Zack dropped his board onto the smooth concrete patio.

"Okay, Zack. You can start by telling us what you took from Alpine Bikes that got Rick Torres fired," Joe said firmly.

Zack didn't answer immediately. Instead, he looked away and put one sneakered foot on the tail of his board. There was an uncomfortable silence. From the expression on Zack's face, it looked as if he wasn't sure where to start. Frank wanted to press him for answers, but his detective's instincts told him to be patient.

Finally, Zack began to speak to the Hardys.

Just then, Frank spotted a black-clad figure jump off the fence surrounding Zack's backyard. With a thump, he landed in the grass about fifteen feet from the pool.

In a second, Frank recognized the figure as the mystery skater from the day before. He saw Zack turn and heard him gasp as he spotted the skater. Before Frank or Joe could react, the helmeted black clad figure dashed over to Zack and pushed him hard.

"Help!" Zack yelled as he started to fall backward over the edge of the empty pool.

5 Cat and Mouse

"Zack!" Joe cried, rushing over to the shallow end of the pool where he lay.

Frank was about to follow when he saw the mystery boarder bend down and scoop up Zack's skateboard. Without stopping for a second, he sprinted across the concrete patio and disappeared down the brick walk toward the front of the house.

"Don't worry about me!" Zack cried. "Just get my board back!"

Frank raced down the walk to the front of the house, with Joe following behind. When they got to the street, the man in black was nowhere in sight.

Suddenly, Frank heard the sound of a motorcycle revving up behind the fence at the back of the house.

"Come on," Frank cried.

They took off at a run, reaching the side of the house just as the man on the motorcycle zoomed past them and bounced off the sidewalk onto the street.

"Let's go!" Joe shouted to his brother as he raced for the van. "That guy's not going to get away this time!"

Frank reached the van seconds after Joe had climbed inside and started the engine.

"Let's nail that guy!" Frank shouted as he pulled open the door and dove into the passenger seat.

"What about Zack?" Joe asked as he zoomed backward out of the driveway.

Frank looked out his window and saw Zack heading for the dirt bike parked in the driveway. "He's coming with us," Frank replied with a grin.

The black-clad man already had a considerable lead on the van, but Frank knew that his brother could catch up to him. Joe pressed down on the accelerator, and the dark blue van took off.

Frank glanced in the passenger-side mirror and saw that Zack was behind them on the dirt bike, gaining steadily. Looking through the windshield, Frank saw the motorcycle several blocks ahead of them, agilely zipping around cars.

"I'm surprised that guy hasn't turned off on a side street to try and shake us," Frank commented.

"I won't lose him," Joe said without taking his eyes off the road.

Zack pulled up next to the passenger side of the

van and shouted, "How are we going to catch that guy?"

"We'll try to trap him between us," Frank shouted back. "Follow our lead."

Zack gave Frank a thumbs-up sign, then leaned low over his handlebars, concentrating on the street ahead.

Birch Street ran straight downhill. Luckily, the traffic was light, so the Hardys had little trouble keeping the black-clad biker in sight. Joe had the accelerator to the floor and was slowly gaining on the thief.

Just then, the biker made a sharp left turn, and Frank realized that he was headed for the Bayport Shopping Mall.

"We've got to catch that guy before he gets to the mall," Frank shouted to Joe. "Once we're in the parking lot, there'll be too much traffic to stop him."

"I know," Joe said in frustration. He cut around an old sedan, and Frank saw that there was no other traffic on the two blocks that lay ahead.

"See if you can pick up some speed," Frank urged.

"I'll give it my best shot," Joe replied, shoving the accelerator all the way to the floor. There was a burst of speed that put the van even with the motorcycle.

The man in black started in surprise as he saw the van pull up along his right side. Joe threw the steering wheel to the left to try to force him off the

44

street. But the man on the bike darted away from the van without losing any speed.

"This guy's good," Joe muttered from between clenched teeth.

Joe tried the same maneuver a second time, and the biker darted away again. But a moment later, he was back beside the van.

Frank caught a flash of something that gleamed brightly in the biker's hand. Suddenly, the man swung the object through the air, and it clanged heavily against Joe's side of the van.

"He's got a chain!" Frank shouted. "Watch out, Joe."

Joe immediately steered the van away from the biker.

The biker bore in close again and lashed out at the van. One of his blows struck the windshield, making a big crack across it from top to bottom.

Joe threw the wheel hard to the left, almost colliding with the biker. Frank glanced at the intersection ahead and was relieved to see that the light was green.

The biker maneuvered ahead of the van and shot across the intersection first. The Hardys' van was only a car length behind him. Wondering if Zack was still with them, Frank looked in the passenger side mirror and saw that he was hot on their tail, a look of determination on his face.

The black-clad biker made a sharp left turn as he entered the mall parking lot. Joe hit the brakes and cut the steering wheel to the left. The van skidded for a moment and rocked up on two wheels. For a heart-stopping second, Frank was afraid that the van might roll. It made the turn safely, though. The van's two right wheels hit the asphalt with an impact that sent a jolt through Frank's body.

"Nice turn," Frank gasped.

The skateboard thief sped down a long aisle of parked cars.

Up ahead, Frank saw a big delivery truck slowly lumbering across the end of the aisle toward one of the parking lot's exits.

"If he gets around that truck, we may lose him," Frank said urgently.

"I know. I'm going as fast as I can," Joe snapped.

The biker veered toward the rear end of the delivery truck. The truck slowed, blocking the aisle as its driver waited for a break in traffic so he could drive out into the street. Frank watched in alarm as he and Joe moved closer and closer to the truck and the motorcycle.

"Joe—hit the brakes!" he cried.

"He'll get away!" Joe shouted back.

Just then, the truck moved forward a few feet. The man on the motorcycle started to cut around the rear of the truck. Suddenly, the bike went into a skid, and the Hardys saw it slide past the rear of the truck in a shower of sparks. Frank and Joe saw Zack's skateboard go flying out of the biker's saddlebags. The black-clad thief lay on the ground next to his bike.

46

Frank was suddenly thrown forward as Joe slammed on the brakes to avoid colliding with the truck.

Joe threw the van into park. Frank hopped out of the van and ran after Joe toward the fallen rider. The driver of the delivery truck didn't stick around to see what was happening, but pulled out into traffic and zoomed away.

When Joe reached the motorcycle, the black-clad man suddenly sat up and threw the length of chain around Joe's ankles. Frank saw him pull Joe's feet out from under him and watched as Joe toppled backward with a yell. The younger Hardy hit the pavement hard and lay there, stunned. Frank stopped short ten feet from the man in black.

The man rose unsteadily and faced Frank, whirling the chain over his head.

Frank stayed just out of reach, looking for an opening. Suddenly, the stranger darted forward, lashing the chain at Frank's head. Frank blocked the blow with his forearm and winced as the chain whipped around his arm.

Before Frank had a chance to recover, his attacker pulled hard on the chain. Frank was jerked forward, and a gloved fist hit him in the pit of his stomach.

"Ooof!" Frank gasped, as all the wind was knocked out of him. He fell to his knees. The stranger pulled the chain away and drew it back for another blow.

The blow never landed. Frank suddenly heard an amplified voice call out: "You there—in black. Stop where you are!"

The helmeted biker didn't waste a second. He suddenly turned on his heel and took off at a run, before Frank had a chance to react. Frank saw that he had a slight limp in his right leg from the motorcycle spill. But he managed to sprint quickly toward an open loading dock at the rear of the nearest store and disappear through a door marked Service Entrance.

Frank pulled himself to his knees. The blow to his stomach had knocked the wind out of him, and he felt dizzy. He watched in frustration as the guy's back disappeared through the service entrance.

"Rats," he said. "There goes our only lead."

As Frank got to his feet, he turned and saw a white golf cart roll up to him. A heavyset security guard in a gray uniform got out.

"Are you okay, son?" the guard asked as he got out of the cart.

"Yeah," Frank said a bit breathlessly. "Just had the wind knocked out of me."

Just then, Zack came running up carrying his skateboard.

"Where were you, Zack?" Frank asked.

"Sorry, Frank," Zack replied. "I followed you into the lot and saw my skateboard go flying. It rolled quite a ways, and I chased it down. I *had* to make sure my board was safe. I didn't think you and Joe needed any help. It was two against one."

"What's going on here?" the security guard asked in a puzzled voice.

"I'll tell you in a minute," Frank replied. "Let me see how my brother is first."

He headed over to Joe, who was slowly getting to his feet. "I'm okay," he said. "Just a little sore."

"Are you sure?" Frank asked anxiously.

"Positive," Joe nodded as he walked a bit stiffly over to Zack and the security guard. "I just got stunned when that creep pulled my feet out from under me."

"You kids mind telling me what's going on here?" the guard asked.

"The guy dressed in black stole my skateboard," Zack explained. "My friends here were trying to get it back."

"Nobody's seriously hurt, right?" the guard asked again.

Frank and Joe shook their heads.

"That's good," the guard said with relief. "But I'm still going to have to write up a report about all this because that other guy spilled his motorcycle on mall property. You'll have to come with me to the security office."

"But—" Zack started to object.

"I've got to follow the rules, son. Sorry," the guard said.

As he climbed back into his golf cart, he said, "Follow me back to the office."

"Sure thing, officer," Joe said. "But let me park my van first."

While Joe put the van in a parking space, Frank borrowed a pen and a piece of paper from the guard. He walked over to the thief's fallen motorcycle and carefully noted down the make and model of the bike as well as its license number.

It was an hour before the security guard finally finished questioning them. Before leaving the mall, Frank found a pay phone and called Lieutenant Con Riley of the Bayport police. He was sure Con would help with this case, as he had many times in the past.

Seconds after Frank dialed Con's number, a voice came on the line saying, "Lieutenant Riley."

"Hi, Con. This is Frank Hardy."

"What can I do for you, Frank?" Con asked.

"I need you to trace down the owner of a motorcycle for me," Frank told him.

Con sighed. "What are you boys up to this time?"

"We'll fill you in later, Con," Frank promised. "It's nothing serious, really."

There was a long pause at the other end of the line, and Frank could tell that Con was thinking.

"Okay," he finally said. "Give me the information."

"Thanks, Con," Frank said gratefully. He quickly read off the make and model of the street bike, along with its license number.

"I'll see what I can find out," Con told him. "I'll call you later." Then he hung up.

* * *

50

It was late in the afternoon when Zack and the Hardys returned to Zack's house. Zack parked his dirt bike in the empty driveway, and Joe pulled up behind him.

"Now that we got your board back, how about continuing our conversation?" Frank said to Zack as he got out of the van. They'd already wasted a lot of time, and Zack still hadn't explained why someone would be after him or his board.

"Okay," Zack replied without much enthusiasm. "Let's go back to my shop."

Frank and Joe followed Zack down the brick walk to the side entrance of the garage. Zack was a few steps ahead of the Hardys, and as he went through the shop door, Frank heard him shout, "Oh, no! I can't believe it!"

Frank and Joe glanced at each other and then sprinted up to the doorway. The first thing Frank saw was that the workshop door was standing open. He remembered that Zack had closed the door earlier, before they went out into the backyard.

Looking over Joe's shoulder, Frank saw that Zack's workbench was turned over on its side. There were lamps, tools, and broken skateboard parts scattered on the floor from one end of the room to the other.

"My workshop has been totally trashed!" Zack exclaimed.

6 Questions and Answers

"It looks like a hurricane swept through here," Joe said, as he surveyed the debris strewn around Zack's workshop.

"A human hurricane," Frank added.

"Oh, man," Zack moaned as he stood in the middle of his wrecked workshop. He slumped into the only chair that hadn't been overturned and looked up at the Hardys. "How could someone do this to me?"

"That's what we have to find out," Joe said. He noticed that the vandal had ripped down all the coffee cans full of nails, nuts, and bolts that Zack had hung up along one wall. The cushions of Zack's couch and chair had been slashed, and the stuffing

52

thrown on the floor. Even the television screen had been kicked in.

It looked as though anything breakable was deliberately destroyed, Joe thought. But why?

Joe began sifting through the wreckage around the worktable. On the floor was a battered deck, the wooden top part of the skateboard. Kneeling down, Joe picked up the board. Its smooth surface had been splintered by what looked like hammer blows, judging from the round impressions on the surface.

"This must have happened while we were chasing the mystery skater," Joe commented.

"At exactly two-twenty-six P.M.," Frank said from the other end of the workshop.

"How do you know that?" Joe asked in surprise.

Frank answered by holding up Zack's clock radio. Its smashed digital face showed 2:26.

"This tells us one thing about the mystery skater," Frank said. "He doesn't work alone."

"Right," Joe agreed. "He has to have an accomplice. He couldn't have done this at the same time we were chasing him."

Joe stood up and dusted the splinters from his knees. Then he stepped over to Zack and laid a hand on his shoulder. "If you suspect someone, I think you'd better tell us, Zack."

Zack didn't reply immediately. His hands shook as he ran his fingers through his mop of blond hair. After a long pause he said softly, "I-I can't think straight right now."

53

He stood up, brushing Joe's hand off his shoulder. He faced the Hardys and said tensely, "Look . . . would you guys mind clearing out? I feel like I need to be alone."

"We're not going anywhere," Joe said firmly. He sat down on the arm of the slashed-up couch. "At least not until we get some answers from you."

"Look, Zack," Frank said quietly, as he righted an easy chair and sat in it. "If you want to go on like this, with people attacking you and vandalizing your stuff, that's your business."

"But," Joe added, "if you want to catch the creeps who did this, then you have to give us your side of the story."

"How about if you start by telling us *exactly* what you did at Alpine Bikes that got Rick Torres fired?" Frank asked.

As Zack met Frank's eyes, Joe thought the lanky skateboarder looked about as miserable as anyone he'd ever seen. "I'm afraid that if I tell you guys the truth, you won't want anything to do with me," Zack said in a low voice.

"Even if you did steal something from Alpine Bikes, we'll still help you out," Frank said.

Zack managed a small smile. "Thanks, you guys." Then he took a deep breath and said, "Okay, it's true. I stole some stuff from Alpine Bikes before I quit."

Joe let out a long whistle. Zack's confession meant they were getting somewhere, but he wasn't sure he liked hearing that this skater, whom he'd admired and was beginning to consider a friend, was a thief. "What did you take?" he asked.

"A bunch of ceramic ball bearings," Zack said. "It's a new high-tech product. They're almost unbreakable and never need to be lubricated. I also took some pieces of superhard carbon fiber material."

"Why would you want to steal materials like that?" Joe asked in a puzzled voice.

"I wanted them for skateboard parts," Zack explained. "I had a machine shop make a set of skateboard trucks out of the composite material. The ball bearings went inside the trucks."

"It sounds as if you went to an awful lot of trouble to make a fancy skateboard," Frank said curiously.

"Yeah, but now I have trucks that will never wear out. And the ceramic ball bearings won't ever get worn or pitted, and they don't need to be lubricated. The board gives me an incredibly fast, smooth ride. I don't think there's a faster skateboard in the world," Zack finished. Joe heard the excitement in his voice and began to understand why Zack had taken such a big risk. To Zack, being the best skateboarder meant everything.

"Let's get back to Rick Torres. Where does he fit in to this story?" Frank asked.

Zack went over to his battered sofa and sat in it before answering. "It was originally Rick's idea to use all that stuff to build a skateboard. He thought of it first, and he told me about it."

"Why do you think Torres was fired?" Frank asked.

"Mr. Travers knew Rick and I were friends. He probably thought Rick helped me steal the stuff and fired him," Zack said.

"*Did* Rick help you?" Joe asked.

"No," Zack said emphatically. "Rick's too honest for that. Stealing those parts was totally my idea."

"But you let Rick take part of the blame for it," Joe reminded him.

"Yeah, I know," Zack admitted miserably. "And after I heard Rick had gotten fired I was too chicken to tell Travers the truth."

"Well, that could explain Torres's grudge against you," Frank said. "So maybe he's your mystery skater. He's definitely tall enough."

"But if Torres *is* the mystery skater, then who is he working with?" Joe asked.

"What about Barb Myers?" Frank asked. He turned to Zack. "You said she's angry with you."

Zack nodded. "If Rick's the mystery skater, it makes sense that Barb would help him."

"Is Barb Myers's grudge against you serious enough to make her do something like this?" Frank asked, looking around at the mess.

"Probably," Zack answered. "Howling Wheels is a small company. Barb really needs a great team to promote her boards. She thinks I ruined her team's chances of winning any major championships this year because I quit."

Joe nodded. "Maybe she and Rick are out to ruin your chances to win the Thrashathon. He steals your board, and she trashes your place, hoping to upset you enough to withdraw from the competition."

Zack shook his head and sighed. "I guess I'm getting what I deserve after what I did."

"You made a mistake," Frank said gently.

"And someone wants to make you pay," Joe added, looking at the wrecked workshop. "We just have to prove who that someone is."

Zack smiled for the first time since they'd discovered the vandalism. "Thanks, guys. Thanks for not coming down hard on me. I just want to make it right again." He paused. "Meanwhile, I guess I'd better deal with this mess." He knelt down and began scooping nails and screws into a coffee can.

Frank and Joe righted Zack's worktable. Then the three of them continued to pick up the debris strewn around the room. They worked in silence for several minutes before a thought occurred to Joe. He placed a skateboard deck on the worktable, looked over at Zack, and said, "You know, if Rick Torres is the mystery skater, there might be a simple way to get him to lay off you."

Zack looked up from the coffee can he was filling with bolts. "What's that?" he asked eagerly.

"You said you want to make everything right again. So I think you should go and apologize to Rick," Joe replied.

"*What?*" Zack said in disbelief. "Are you crazy? Rick's just waiting for his chance to beat my head in!"

"If it will make it any easier, Joe and I will go with you. We'll make sure you two have a nice, peaceful talk," Frank offered.

"I don't know," Zack said doubtfully.

"Look, Maggie told us you two used to be really tight. Isn't it worth a risk to save a good friendship?" Joe asked.

"But he hates me," Zack replied.

"Maybe it would help if you offered to straighten things out at Alpine Bikes," Frank suggested. "You could tell Travers you stole the parts and offer to pay for them. Then maybe they'd give Rick his old job back."

Zack thought for a moment. "I'd really like to get my best friend back," he said finally.

"Then give our idea a try," Joe urged.

"Okay, I will," Zack said. "I'll call the skating park and see if he's still there."

Zack stood up and went over to the door. Before he went through it, he turned back to Frank and Joe and asked, "But what if Rick isn't the mystery skater?"

"Then we still have a mystery to solve. But at least you'll have your best friend back," Joe replied.

Zack thought about that for a minute, then smiled. "Yeah, that makes sense," he said, leaving the shop to make the call.

After Zack was gone, Joe turned to his brother. "Do you think Torres really is the mystery skater?"

Frank shrugged. "He's the prime suspect."

"I've seen Torres skate on TV. I'm sure he could skate on that skinny wall the way the skater did when he escaped at the park," Joe pointed out.

"Well, if Torres isn't our mystery man, then we'll just have to see what happens after Zack makes up with him," Frank replied. "If he *is* the guy, I'm hoping he'll admit everything to Zack, and then the attacks will stop."

"We'd better hope Rick can get Barb Myers to back off, too," Joe said.

Frank and Joe continued straightening up the workshop until Zack returned a few minutes later.

"Hi, guys," Zack announced when he returned. "Rick left the park to go back to his motel. The woman I talked to said he's staying at the Elm Court. Do you know where that is?"

"We sure do," Joe said, putting down the broom he'd been using. "Let's go!"

The Elm Court Motel was on Mainways Boulevard, only a few blocks down from the new skating park. It was a slightly run-down, two-story building with space for over a hundred guests in its three long wings of rooms.

The desk clerk told the Hardys and Zack that Torres was staying in Room 203, on the upper level. Joe led the way, with Zack nervously following him and Frank bringing up the rear.

When they got to Torres's room, Joe stepped away from Zack. "Go ahead, Zack. It'll be okay," Joe prodded him. "We'll be right behind you."

Zack swallowed hard and nodded. Then he stepped up to the door and knocked on it.

"Yeah, just a minute," a voice called from inside.

Joe heard the sound of the door chain being unlatched. Then the door opened, and Rick Torres stood before them.

The tall, tanned skateboarder took one look at Zack and his face twisted into a mask of anger. Before Joe could stop him, Torres was lunging for Zack. Then Rocket's fingers clutched Zack's shirt and he yanked Zack toward him, so that the two were only inches apart.

"You!" Torres snarled. "You ought to know better than to come here. I ought to kill you after what you've done to me—you back-stabbing little weasel!"

7 Hard Words

Frank saw a shocked look on Zack's face as he and Joe shot forward and grabbed Torres by the arms. After a struggle, they finally pulled Torres away from Zack. Rick was strong, but he was no match for the combined strength of the Hardys.

"Easy, Torres—why don't you relax," Joe warned.

"Let me go, you two goons!" Torres shouted, straining to break free from the Hardys' grasps.

"Calm down," Frank said firmly. "We only came to talk."

"Did you hire those two henchmen to back you up, Zack?" Torres retorted. "Couldn't handle it on your own?"

Zack looked at Torres with a pleading expression. "Please, Rick, let me talk."

Torres stopped struggling against the Hardys. But Frank and his brother continued to hold Rick's arms tightly. They couldn't be sure that Torres wouldn't break free and go after Zack again.

"What do you have to say that's so important, Zack?" Torres snapped.

"I came to square things with you," Zack replied softly.

"It's too late for that!" Torres said hotly.

"Give him a break, Torres," Joe said. "It wasn't easy for him to come here today."

Zack took a step nearer to Torres. "I want us to be friends again. I mean it, Rick. I'll do whatever it takes."

"Oh, yeah?" Torres said sarcastically. "What are you going to do, get me my old job back?"

"I'm going to try," Zack said sincerely. When Torres gave Zack a confused look, Zack went on. "As soon as the Thrashathon is over, I'll call Travers and tell him I was the one who took those parts from the factory. I'll tell him you had nothing to do with it, I swear!"

Zack's words seemed to have a calming effect on Torres. Frank felt the skater relax a bit.

Rocket Rick's face lost its angry hardness. "You'd do that?" he asked suspiciously. "Why? What's in it for you?"

"Nothing," Zack replied firmly. "And I'll probably get into a lot of trouble with Alpine Bikes, but I don't care. I'll tell Travers that I'll pay for everything I stole."

Frank heard a sound behind him. He turned and saw several people standing in the motel hallway, looking at the four of them curiously.

"Maybe we'd better take this conversation inside," Frank suggested. "I think we're attracting a little too much attention."

"How about it, Rick?" Zack asked. "Can we come inside?"

"Yeah, I guess so," Torres replied after a moment. "Let go of me," he snapped at the Hardys.

Frank and Joe took their hands off Torres, and the burly, dark-haired thrasher turned on his heel and walked back into his room. Frank stepped through the doorway after him, followed by Joe and Zack. Inside, Frank cleared a pile of safety pads off a chair and sat down. Joe sat on top of a low bureau, while Zack leaned against the room's door.

Even though Zack wanted to square things with Torres, the Hardys still had to find out if he was the mystery skater. Frank looked around the room to see if any of the clothes lying around matched the black shirt and pants of the mystery skater. He didn't spot any items of clothing that matched up. But he knew Torres could have easily stashed the clothes and helmet in the dresser or closet.

"So, why do you want to make friends all of a sudden, Zack?" Torres asked as he sat on the edge of his unmade bed.

63

"I feel lousy about what happened, Rick," Zack replied. "I never meant for you to get fired."

"Maybe not," Torres said. "But the fact is, I did get canned. Once Travers discovered those high-tech parts were missing, he wouldn't believe me even though I swore I was innocent. I needed that job, Zack."

"I know," Zack said miserably. "But I promise that I'll tell Travers the truth just as soon as the Thrashathon is over."

"Yeah, sure," Torres said with a sarcastic laugh. "I'll believe that when it happens. What did you do with those parts, anyway?" Rick asked with curiosity. "They could be used to make one incredible skateboard."

Zack didn't meet Rick's eye. "I guess they could," he said.

Frank waited for Zack to confess that was exactly what he did with the parts, but the teen thrasher held back the information.

After a long pause, Torres said, "Just because we're making up doesn't mean I'm going to hold back in the competition, you know."

Zack grinned. "Course not. I'd feel let down if you weren't out there trying as hard as you could to beat me. But as soon as the competition is over, I swear I'm going to get you your job back."

"Okay, we've got a deal," Torres said, grabbing Zack's hand and pumping it.

"Great, man," Zack said with a big grin. "You won't regret this."

"I'd better not," Torres warned playfully. "I'm taking a big chance trusting you after what you did to me."

"Guys, I don't mean to butt in, but there's something else we need to talk about," Frank said seriously.

"What's that?" Torres asked.

"Do you know about that skater who attacked Zack yesterday?" Joe asked.

"Yeah," Torres replied, nodding his head. "There was quite a buzz about that guy in the skate park, but I didn't see him."

"He wasn't just at the park, Rick," Frank said. "He showed up at Zack's house today and tried to steal his board."

"Oh, yeah?" Torres looked surprised.

"And while we were out getting it back, someone else trashed Zack's workshop," Joe added.

"Man, what a bummer," Torres said. He shook his head and shrugged. "Looks like you've got trouble, Zack."

"Where were *you* yesterday afternoon, Rick?" Joe asked pointedly.

Torres was startled by the question. He looked around the room at the three teens. "Hey, you guys don't think that mystery skater was *me*, do you?" He laughed nervously.

"It occurred to us," Joe replied. "You're a good enough skater to pull off an escape like the one that guy made."

"Look," Torres told them indignantly, "I didn't

65

even get into Bayport until yesterday afternoon. And I was at the park practicing all day today. I just got back here a little while ago."

"Can you prove that?" Frank said evenly.

"Yeah," Torres replied. "There were dozens of people who saw me there. Barb Myers, for one, and the guys from the Zebra Boards team, and a bunch of other skaters. Just ask around at the park."

"We will," Joe assured him. "First thing tomorrow."

"What about that stunt you pulled at the park earlier today?" Frank asked. "You could have hurt Zack."

Rick smiled at first, then frowned. "Barb put me up to it. But I didn't hurt anyone." Torres turned to Zack and looked him right in the eye. "Sorry, bro."

"You're forgiven," Zack said. "But watch out in the competition. I'm still a better thrasher, dude," he said with a laugh.

"We'll see about that," Rick countered.

Although the two thrashers had made up, Frank wasn't convinced that Torres was innocent. He still could be the mystery skater. Frank made a mental note to check out Torres's alibi.

Torres yawned wide and stretched. "Well, if that's everything, do you mind leaving now? I'm in training, and I have to hit the sack early."

"Sure, no problem," Frank said, as he stood up and started for the door.

"See you around the park, Rocket," Zack said as he followed Frank and Joe out the door.

"You guys believe him, don't you?" Zack asked the Hardys as they headed toward the van.

"He sounds sincere," Frank admitted. "But we need to check his story and a few other details before we can rule him out as a suspect." He paused after they got in the van. "Why didn't you tell Rick the truth about what you did with those parts?" he asked.

Joe waited for Zack to answer. The teen thrasher ran his hands through his long blond hair and made a face. "I don't know. Maybe there's a part of me that wants to trust Rick more than I really do. But if my deal comes through, I'm going to tell Rick everything, and split the money with him fifty-fifty. No point in telling him about it until it happens."

"What deal are you talking about?" Joe asked as Frank pulled the van into traffic.

Zack hesitated for a moment. "I guess I might as well tell you guys. I have a tentative deal with one of the big skateboard companies to mass-produce copies of my board," Zack told him. "That's why the Thrashathon is so important to me, and why I have to keep a hold on my board. When everyone sees what the board can do, they'll be amazed."

"Who's the deal with?" Frank asked, keeping his eyes on traffic.

Zack paused, and Frank could sense his reluctance to share this information. Then Zack said, "It's with Chris Hall's outfit, Scorpion Boards. Chris really wants to make the deal, but we still have to work out the details."

67

"Scorpion Boards, huh? A deal like that could mean a lot of money," Joe said.

"Yeah, it might," Zack said, "but I don't want you to tell *anybody* about it. I have another deal I'm working on, too, and the whole thing might get blown if any information gets out."

"What's the other deal all about?" Frank asked.

"Well, I'd rather not say. . . ." Zack replied, avoiding Frank's eyes.

Frank sighed. "Look, Zack, we can't help you if you're not going to tell us everything. We need to know about this deal before—"

"Listen," Zack interrupted. "I have a way to make it up to Fred Travers for what I did. It's a plan I've got cooking in my head, but I can't tell anyone about it. If word gets to the wrong people, the whole thing might not go down."

Joe spoke up from the back of the van. "I don't know about you, Zack. You've got an awful lot of secrets."

"Well, this is one secret you're not going to learn," Zack said, a grin appearing wide on his face. "It's going to make me rich. And when Rick gets his fifty percent, he won't even need that job at Alpine."

After dropping Zack at his house and making plans to meet up the next day, Frank pointed the van in the direction of the Hardys' house.

"What do you think about Zack?" Joe asked his brother.

"Another secret," Frank said, shaking his head.

68

"I'm beginning to wonder if we're working for the right side here."

"I know what you mean," Joe said. "But he did try to make amends with Rick, I'll give him that." Joe looked at his brother. "You still don't trust Torres, do you?"

Frank shook his head. "Not until we check him out and see if he was really at the park all day. It'd be great if he were telling the truth, though."

"Except then we wouldn't have a clue about who's after Zack," Joe said. "Hey, I'm starving. How about stopping off to get a pizza. A big one, with everything on it."

"Mom left us meat loaf, like she always does when she's out of town," Frank reminded him. He hoped his parents and Aunt Gertrude were having a good time on their vacation.

"But after all that detective action today," Frank added, "I think we deserve something tastier than leftover meat loaf!"

Half an hour later, they returned home with the pizza. Frank and Joe grabbed some sodas and headed into the study to eat and watch TV. When they entered the room, Frank saw the message light blinking on the answering machine. He hit the replay button and heard Con Riley's voice coming from the speaker a moment later.

"Hello, Frank. This is Con Riley. I ran down the license number you gave me. The motorbike belongs to a man named Edward Bordenka. He lives at Ten-forty-three Mainways Boulevard. He reported

69

that the bike was stolen today around noon. I hope this helps. You and Joe stay out of trouble, okay?"

Frank hung up, feeling disappointed on hearing the news. "I was hoping the motorcycle our mystery friend left at the mall would lead us to his identity. But since the bike was stolen, it's not much of a lead."

"It was worth a shot," Joe pointed out. "The motorcycle was stolen from the neighborhood around the skating park. Maybe that mystery skater lives near there."

"Maybe, maybe not," Frank replied. He opened the pizza box and picked up a slice. "But right now, I just want to concentrate on eating."

It wasn't long before Frank and Joe were down to the last slice of pizza. Joe stifled a huge yawn as he reached for it. Frank felt as though he could fall asleep any minute.

"You know," Frank said with a yawn, "I thought we could keep talking about the case, but I'm just too tired."

"Me, too," Joe said. "Why don't we call it a night and make a fresh start in the morning?"

"Good idea," Frank agreed. "If I don't get to bed soon I'm going to fall asleep right here on the sofa."

Upstairs, Frank fell asleep almost as soon as his head hit the pillow. He slept uneasily, and a strange smell kept creeping into his dreams.

The odor grew stronger until finally it woke him up. He sat up groggily. The smell from his dream was still there, and he had a splitting headache.

70

He stood up and immediately felt dizzy. He sat on the edge of his bed with his head between his hands, trying to clear his thoughts.

He coughed. The odor in the air was choking him, keeping him from getting enough oxygen. Frank started to nod off again, then jerked awake. With a shock, he realized what the smell was.

Gas!

8 Zack Takes a Fall

With a sudden chill of fear, Frank dragged himself awake. Unless he opened some windows and turned off the gas—fast!—he and Joe were going to suffocate.

Frank staggered over to his bedroom window and threw it open. He leaned out and drew in several deep breaths. The night air revived him, and he felt his head clearing.

Taking one more deep breath, Frank pulled his head back through the window. As he walked through his room and down the hall, Joe's room appeared to be a million miles away. Frank was dizzy and light-headed, and his knees almost buckled more than once before he finally reached Joe's room.

Frank steadied himself against the wall. "Joe!" he called out. "Wake up!"

Without waiting for an answer, Frank staggered into the room and headed straight for one of the windows. After opening it and taking another deep breath of fresh air, he hurried over to the bed.

"Come on, Joe, wake up!" he urged, shaking his brother by the shoulder.

"Wha—what's going on?" Joe mumbled. He opened his eyes and squinted at his brother through the dim light.

Frank grabbed Joe under the arms and pulled him up to a sitting position.

"I'm awake—I'm awake," Joe managed to say. "What's going on?" he muttered. "Is something wrong?"

"You bet there is," Frank cried. He led Joe from his bed to the open window and stuck his brother's head into the fresh air. "The house is full of gas!"

"Hey," Joe said, banging his head on the window frame. "Take it easy." He took in a deep breath of fresh air, turned to his brother and said, "What do you mean, the house is full of gas?"

"Smell," Frank told him, sniffing the air.

Joe did, then gave his brother a nod that told him he was right. "We've got to get downstairs and turn it off."

"Come on," Frank said, leading the way out of Joe's bedroom. As Joe followed Frank, he grabbed a couple of bandannas off the top of his bureau. He handed one to Frank and wrapped the other around

73

his nose and mouth. The gas stung his eyes as he and his brother made their way down the stairs. Joe began to have trouble breathing, and he felt himself getting light-headed.

When they reached the bottom of the stairs, Frank motioned toward the living room. "Open some windows while I get the stove," he gasped.

His eyes burning from the gas fumes, Frank went into the kitchen. As he turned off the switches on the stove, he saw that the pilot lights were all out. Frank's lungs began to ache for fresh air as he stumbled over to the kitchen windows and threw them open.

To get even more air into the kitchen, Frank went to open the back door. When he reached down, he realized with a shock that the door was unlocked. Frank was positive he'd locked it before leaving the house that morning. They'd left and come back through the front door.

"Hey, Joe," Frank called out. "Come take a look at this."

Joe came into the kitchen from the living room, stepped over to the back door, and knelt down to examine the doorknob.

"Someone broke in," Joe confirmed. He knelt beside his brother and peered at the lock cylinder on the outside part of the doorknob. The porch light was bright enough for both Hardys to make out scratches in the metal all around the key-hole.

"Looks like that lock was picked, all right," Joe

said. "Whoever did it must have been a real pro, too. Neither of us heard a thing."

Frank stood up, a thoughtful expression on his face. "This case is getting serious. Whoever broke in tonight was trying to kill us."

"Our mystery skater?" Joe suggested.

Frank nodded. "He probably knows we're helping Zack, and he's trying to get us out of the way.

"You know," Frank continued after a moment, "I thought at first this whole thing with Zack was just a simple case of harassment," Frank said as he went to the sink to fill a glass with water. "But if Zack's enemies are willing to kill us to get us off the case, there's got to be something more at stake."

"It must have something to do with Zack's souped-up skateboard," Joe said. "The mystery skater tried to steal it twice. He would have gotten away with it the last time if we hadn't been there to chase him."

"But if it's Zack's board his enemies are after, why would they bother to trash his workshop?" Frank wondered.

"Maybe Zack's enemies tried a double-pronged attack," Joe said suddenly. "The mystery skater made a grab for the board, which pulled us away from the shop. That would give the skater's accomplice time to search the shop for a spare board or maybe more of those parts that Zack used."

"That's not a bad theory, Joe, except how could they know for sure that Zack *had* an extra board or spare parts?" Frank asked.

Joe shrugged. "Maybe they didn't. Maybe searching his shop was just a shot in the dark. And when the burglar couldn't find anything, he or she got frustrated and trashed the place."

Frank yawned and rubbed his forehead. "What do you say we sleep on it? Tomorrow we can head over to the skate park and see if Torres's alibi checks out."

"I like that plan, especially the part about sleeping on it," Joe said, catching Frank's yawn.

The next morning, Frank and Joe ate a quick breakfast before getting in their van to head for the park. As Frank started up the van, Joe reminded him that they'd promised Zack they'd pick him up on their way. Frank pulled out of the driveway and made a detour toward Zack's house.

While Frank parked the van outside the Michaelses' house, Joe noticed that the house across the street was still vacant—except that he could have sworn he saw a face appear in an upstairs window.

"Frank," he said to his brother, "turn around really slowly. Tell me if you see anything in the upstairs window of that house," he said.

Frank turned around, looked for a moment, then turned back to Joe. "I don't see a thing," Frank said. "What's up?"

Joe turned to look again. The window was empty. "I must be seeing things," he said. "But I thought for sure there was a face in that window."

Frank laughed and climbed out of the van. "Maybe it's an aftereffect from last night's gas."

"Right," Joe said, following his brother to Zack's workshop. He looked at the window again, but there still wasn't anyone there. He closed his eyes and shook his head, trying to clear the fuzzy feeling and the leftover throbbing at his temples. Maybe his brother was right.

Zack grinned from ear to ear when he saw the Hardys. "Check it out," he said. "Everything's back to the way it was."

Despite his cheerful voice and smile, Joe noticed that Zack looked tired. Looking around the shop, Joe saw that everything was back in place. All of Zack's tools had been hung up, and the skateboard decks, wheels, trucks, and axles were stowed away in their bins along one wall.

Zack picked up his board from the worktable and examined it closely. "In fact, I just finished making some adjustments to my board. Wanna see me try it out?"

Before Frank or Joe could answer, Zack was out the door of his workshop, heading down the path toward the Michaelses' empty swimming pool. With a shrug, Frank and Joe followed the thrasher.

When they got to the pool area, Zack was already performing freestyle stunts on the smooth surface around the pool.

"Awright!" the thrasher yelled. "It's even better than before!"

Joe watched as Zack dismounted. But Zack

wasn't finished performing. He leaned heavily on the skateboard's rear end with his left foot, bringing its nose up into the air. Then, still keeping his weight on the rear of the board, Zack brought his right foot up, balanced on the nose of the board, and spun around on the rear wheels. Joe began to feel dizzy just from watching him.

Finally, Zack shifted his weight to the front of the board, slamming the front wheels down right at the edge of the pool.

"Now watch me catch some side air," Zack said with a grin.

"Aren't you going to put on your helmet and pads first?" Frank asked.

"Negative," Zack said with a shake of his head. "I don't need safety gear in my own pool."

Frank rolled his eyes at Joe. And even though Joe was in awe of Zack's ability, he couldn't help feeling that the thrasher was a little overconfident.

"You really shouldn't skate without safety gear," Joe reminded him.

Zack made a face. "I know what I'm doing." He shifted his board backward with a jerk, then shot over the lip of the pool and down the slope of the shallow end.

"Carve large, Zack!" Joe shouted. As he and Frank watched closely, Zack zoomed down into the deep end of the pool and shifted his weight to the tail of his board. Then, all of a sudden, the skateboard began to slip out from under his feet.

"Whoa!" Zack shouted as he fought to keep his

78

balance. The nose of the board popped into the air, and its front wheels hit the side of the pool.

As soon as Zack's board hit the pool wall, the thrasher lost his balance completely. The board shot out from under his feet and went flying in the air.

"Yeeow!" Zack cried out, discovering only empty space below him.

Joe watched helplessly. There was absolutely no way he could help Zack. His arms flying, Zack struggled to prevent the fall. But Joe knew it was no use.

"Help me!" Zack cried, as his right shoulder slammed against the pool's concrete wall.

9 A Break in the Case

"Zack!" Joe shouted, running toward the edge of the pool.

Joe jumped into the pool at the shallow end and raced toward Zack. When Joe was fifteen feet away from him he suddenly began to slide. His arms flailed in the air wildly as he struggled to keep his balance.

It was no use. Joe's feet slid out from under him and he fell backward. "Oof!" he gasped as he landed hard on his rear end. He caught his breath and placed one hand on the floor of the pool for balance. As he looked up, Joe saw his brother climbing down the ladder. Zack was still lying on the floor, clutching his shoulder and moaning in pain.

"Be careful," Joe warned his brother. "The bottom is really slippery."

Frank nodded as he stepped off the ladder. When Frank reached the middle of the pool, Joe saw his brother's feet slide out from under him. Frank held out his arms to try to steady himself and skidded sideways. Then he slid down past Joe, finally stopping at the deep end of the pool near Zack.

Keeping both hands pressed tightly against the side of the pool, Joe inched down the sloping floor toward Zack, one step at a time. Finally, he reached Frank and Zack, who lay against the pool wall with his eyes closed.

Frank knelt down next to Zack. The thrasher looked up at him and opened his eyes, his face filled with pain.

"My shoulder," Zack gasped. "I think it's broken."

Frank nodded. "Don't try to move," he said. "I'll call for an ambulance. You stay here with Zack while I get the ambulance," he told his brother.

Frank stood up slowly. Slipping and sliding on the pool floor, he made his way to the ladder and climbed up.

Joe watched Frank run over to the sliding glass doors at the rear of the Michaelses' house. Then he turned to Zack and said reassuringly, "The ambulance should be here soon."

"I hope so," Zack replied, wincing with pain. "My shoulder hurts like crazy."

"The ambulance is on its way!" Joe suddenly heard Frank call from the house.

"Great!" Joe called back.

"Would you have Frank call my mom or dad?" Zack asked. "Their work numbers are by the phone. He should tell them I'm hurt, and let them know what hospital I'm going to."

"Sure thing," Joe replied. "Just take it easy, okay?"

"I can't do anything else," Zack replied with a grim smile.

Joe crawled over to the side of the pool and passed Zack's message on to Frank.

After a few minutes Frank returned to the pool. "It's all taken care of, Zack," he said as he sat on the top rung of the ladder. "Your mom's meeting you at Bayport General Hospital."

"The bottom of the pool is definitely coated with something. What do you think this stuff is?" Joe asked, running his hand along the pool's slick surface.

"I don't know," Frank admitted. "Some kind of oil or lubricant."

"What I'm wondering is how the person who did this could have gotten to the pool if Zack was home," Joe said.

"I haven't left the house since yesterday. I was working in the shop all night and all this morning," Zack said.

"Were you using any power tools to repair your shop?" Frank asked.

Wincing a little, Zack nodded. "Yeah, I was using a drill, a sander, and the vacuum cleaner."

Frank looked at Joe. "Zack's tools would have covered any noise our mystery friend made." He shook his head in frustration. "I just wish I could figure out how Zack's enemies know when to strike."

Joe thought for a moment. Then he remembered the vacant house across the street, and that he thought he had seen a face in one of the upstairs windows. He was about to remind his brother when the wail of an approaching siren cut the air. Seconds later, Joe heard an ambulance screech to a halt in front of the Michaelses' home. Then two paramedics came running around the side of the house.

Frank warned the paramedics about the slick coating, and he and Joe waited as the man and woman helped Zack out of the pool. They put his arm in a temporary sling, then strapped Zack into a wheeled stretcher.

Joe rolled Zack's skateboard over to the ladder and handed it up to Frank. Then he climbed up out of the pool. The Hardys walked over to Zack just as the paramedics were about to wheel him away.

"Can we do anything else for you?" Joe asked Zack.

"Hang on to my board for me," Zack begged them. "Guard it with your lives. Oh, yeah, and lock up the house and my shop."

"We will," Frank replied.

"Don't worry, Zack. No one's getting this board away from us," Joe assured him.

As soon as the paramedics had taken Zack away, Frank and Joe returned to the pool. Frank was about to climb back inside it when Joe said, "Remember that vacant house across the street?"

"The one that's haunted, you mean?" Frank joked.

Joe made a face at his brother. "Maybe I *wasn't* seeing things," he said. "Maybe the mystery skater or his accomplice is using the house to keep an eye on Zack."

Frank thought for a moment. "You know, you could be right. Let's check it out after I get a sample of the goop in this pool."

Frank climbed down the ladder, stepping carefully onto the slippery pool floor. Joe watched as his brother knelt down to examine the bottom more closely.

"This stuff sure feels weird," Frank commented. "Joe, can you find me a clean jar from Zack's shop?"

"Sure," Joe replied. He turned and headed for the shop. Moments later, he returned with an empty jar. "Here, catch," he said, tossing the jar to his brother.

Frank caught it, then crawled to the drain at the bottom of the pool. He scraped off some of the slick film with his pocketknife and carefully put it in the jar.

"What are you doing?" Joe called down to his brother.

"I need a sample of this stuff so we can find out what it is," Frank explained.

"How are you going to do that?" Joe asked in a puzzled tone.

"I'll bring it to a hardware store on the way home. It smells like something familiar, but I'm not sure what."

"Let's lock up the house and the shop," Joe said, "then we can check out that vacant house."

Before they headed across the street, Joe stopped by their van so he could hide Zack's skateboard in the back under a pile of blankets. Then he locked the van and joined his brother.

The Hardys walked across the street to the pale green two-story house.

Joe looked up and down the block to make sure there were no neighbors watching. Then he squatted down to examine the lock on the front door. He saw that the gleaming brass lock cylinder wasn't scratched up. "This lock doesn't look like it's been picked," Joe told Frank.

"Let's try the back door," Frank suggested. "If someone's trying to slip in and out of the house unseen, they're more likely to do it from the back."

Frank and Joe walked around the side of the vacant house to the backyard gate. Like Zack's house, the vacant house had a tall fence surrounding the backyard.

"I hope none of the neighbors think we're burglars and call the police," Joe commented.

"That's all we'd need today," Frank said. "Getting hauled downtown to explain to Con Riley why we were sneaking into a locked house."

When they reached the back door, Frank and Joe examined the lock. They saw the same kind of scratches around the keyhole that they'd seen on the back door at their own house.

"This one's definitely been picked," Joe said.

"Is the door unlocked?" Frank asked.

Joe tried the door. It was locked.

"Give me a minute and I'll get us inside," Frank said.

Frank pulled a credit card from his wallet, poked the card through the narrow space between the door frame and the lock, and wiggled it. A moment later, Joe heard the lock click open.

"After you," Frank said with a smile as he turned the knob and held the door open.

Joe closed the door behind him after they went in. The house smelled musty, as if it hadn't been aired out in a long time.

"Looks empty," Joe whispered. "But I think we should check it out, anyway."

Frank nodded. "Yeah, let's start upstairs."

They started up the stairs. Joe paused before reaching the second floor landing, listening for sounds of movement. He heard nothing, so he went on to the second floor. Frank followed, moving as quietly as he could.

The first and second rooms they checked were empty. But the door to the third room was closed. Joe pushed the door open slowly. The room was empty. Frank and Joe stepped inside. Joe opened the closet door. There was nothing in the closet except for a few hangers. There was only one window in the room, which looked down on Zack's house and gave a perfect view of the windows in Zack's garage workshop.

On the floor under the window, Joe spotted several crumpled paper coffee cups and a half-eaten roast beef sandwich.

"Looks like we found somebody's stakeout spot," Joe said quietly.

Frank took a handkerchief out of his pocket. He carefully picked up one of the coffee cups and wrapped it in the handkerchief. "Maybe we can get some fingerprints off it," he told his brother.

"What do we do now?" Joe asked.

"I think we should tell Con Riley what's been happening," Frank said. "Let's leave everything else in the room untouched. Con may want to send a squad to dust for fingerprints."

"Good idea," Joe agreed. He looked down at the trash, making sure there wasn't a clue there they were missing. Kicking at the pile with his foot, Joe noticed another paper cup—except this one seemed to have a smudge along the edge. He picked it up. Sure enough, there was a dark red mark on the top of the cup.

"Looks like lipstick," Frank said.

"Barb Myers," Joe concluded.

Frank nodded. "Just what I was thinking. Although we can't be sure."

"I know, but she could be after Zack's board," Joe said. He knew that Barb owned Howling Wheels and that her company didn't have much money. If she got hold of Zack's skateboard, it could bring her a lot of cash.

"It's a distinct possibility," Frank said. "We'll know more when we dust this cup for fingerprints."

"But if she doesn't have a record," Joe reminded him, "the prints on the cup won't help us much. Also, it doesn't explain who Barb's accomplice is. You know she couldn't be the mystery skater— she's too short."

Joe and Frank exchanged a look. They both knew the next logical connection.

"Torres," Joe said softly.

Frank let out a long sigh. "He could be working with her, it's true. Myers could have convinced Rick to steal Zack's board, use it in the competition, then let her have it to see how it was designed."

"But Rick really did seem happy to make things up with Zack," Joe pointed out. "You think Rick could have been fooling him?"

Frank shrugged. "Let's just head home. We'll stop at the hardware store on the way."

"We should call the real estate agent who handles this house, too," Joe suggested. "If we tell him he's had trespassers here, maybe he'll put better locks on the doors."

"Good thinking, Joe," Frank said. "That should keep whoever's been spying on Zack out of business —for a while at least."

"And give us time to figure out who it is," Joe added, closing the door and following Frank downstairs. After leaving through the same gate they'd entered, Frank stopped by the sign in the front yard. He quickly jotted down the name and phone number of the real estate agent. Then they headed across the street to their van.

While Frank brought the jar into the hardware store to determine what was in it, Joe picked up some hero sandwiches for lunch in a deli across the street.

When they both got back in the van Joe looked at his brother and said, "From the expression you're wearing I guess you're not too happy."

"I'm not," Frank said bluntly. "I thought the goop from Zack's pool would be some kind of lead, but it's just another dead end."

"Why, what is it?"

"The manager in the store said it's a silicone-based industrial lubricant," Frank replied.

"Do you have any idea what it might be used for? That might give us some clue about where it came from."

"Forget it, Joe," Frank said with a sigh. "This stuff is used whenever a petroleum lubricant won't do the job. If you use regular oil on plastic gears, it would cause them to decompose."

"Where can you buy it?" Joe asked.

"The manager said you can buy it anywhere— auto parts stores, hardware stores," Frank answered glumly. "Too many places to trace down."

Back at their house, the Hardys began eating their lunch. Wasting no time, Joe called the real estate agent and told him about the trespassers. The agent thanked him for the call and assured Joe that all the doors on the house would be padlocked. Joe hung up the phone. He was about to pick it up again to call Con, when the phone began to ring.

"Hello, Joe Hardy speaking," Joe said into the receiver.

"Hi, Joe," said a familiar voice. "This is Zack."

"Zack! How are you feeling?" Joe asked.

"Not so good, Joe," Zack said sadly. "I cracked my shoulder blade in that fall. The doctor says I can't compete in the Thrashathon."

"Oh, no!" Joe said with a groan. "What are you going to do?"

There was a long pause at the other end of the line. "Well, uh, I was thinking," Zack said, hesitating. "It's really important for me to show off my board."

"I know, Zack." Joe felt awful for the thrasher. "It really stinks that you can't ride it."

There was another long pause. Finally, Zack spoke up. "I can't. But you can."

"What?" Joe asked. "What are you talking about? The only way I could ride your board—"

"Is if I asked you," Zack finished for him. "What would you say, Joe," the thrasher asked, "to being the first-ever replacement for Zack 'the Hawk' Michaels in Bayport's Thrashathon?"

10 Tricky Business

"No way!" Joe exclaimed. "You want me to skate for you? I'm just an amateur. There's no way I could win."

"You're a good skater," Zack said. "You can use my board, and I'll give you some pointers." He paused for a moment, then said, "Look, Joe, this is your first competition. It doesn't matter if you win. I'll be coaching you, so in a way, it'll be like I'm out there competing, too. Chris Hall needs to see what my board can do. This is important to me. So, will you skate?"

Joe was growing more excited as he thought about using Zack's board in the national competition, and going up against people like Rick Torres and Danny Hayashi. How could he refuse?

"You've got a deal!" Joe couldn't keep the excitement from his voice. "And thanks for asking me. It means a lot!"

"Listen," Zack said, "I'm getting released from here in a few minutes. How about meeting me at the park in an hour?"

"Sounds great!" Joe agreed.

Joe hung up the phone and quickly told his brother about his conversation with Zack.

"Are you sure you can do this?" Frank asked. "You're pretty good for an amateur skater, but do you think you're up to competing with the pros?"

"I'll give it my best shot," Joe said. "Besides, I'll be using Zack's board, and Zack's going to coach me."

"But you only have the rest of today to practice," Frank pointed out. "The Thrashathon starts tomorrow at noon."

"I know," Joe replied. "I'm meeting Zack at the park for a coaching session in an hour."

"It's a gutsy thing to do, Joe," Frank said, shaking his head. "Especially with that mystery skater still on the loose, looking to steal Zack's board."

Joe frowned. In all the excitement about skating in Zack's place, he'd almost forgotten they still had a mystery to solve. Then he had an idea.

"Hey, Frank," he said. "Since we're pretty sure it's Zack's board the mystery skater is after, maybe he'll come after it again. Only this time, I won't let him get away."

93

"Yes, but what if he *does* get away—and with Zack's board?"

"I've already thought of that," Joe said. "While I practice I'm going to borrow an idea from surfers. I'll tie a nylon safety line to a hook near the end of the board, then attach the cord to my wrist or ball it up in my fist. Even if the mystery skater knocks me off the board, he won't get very far with it."

"Unless he cuts your safety line," Frank pointed out. "That also sounds dangerous. What if you get tangled up in the cord or it trips you up?"

Joe shrugged. "I'm going to use a fairly short line and keep my moves simple."

"It might work, I guess," Frank said doubtfully.

"At the worst it'll slow the mystery boarder down long enough for you or me to catch him," Joe added.

"Worth a try," Frank said. "We should dust these cups for prints, then head over to the park. I still haven't checked out Torres's alibi."

Joe made a face. "I know. It kills me to think it might be Torres who's after Zack's board," he said, finishing his hero.

"You said it," Frank agreed. "You call Con Riley while I handle the fingerprints, then we can get going."

Joe picked up the phone as Frank headed downstairs to feed the image from the prints into the computer and set up an online search through the police data base. He knew the search would take some time, but if the computer found a match, the

94

information would be waiting for them when they got back from the park.

Meanwhile Joe let the police officer know about what he and Frank had found at the empty house across from Zack's. When Joe was done, he found Frank downstairs shutting down the computer.

"Riley said he'd send some people over to check out that house for fingerprints," Joe said. "But he wants us to come down to the station sometime soon and make statements about the attacks on Zack and the gas attack the other night."

"Well, let's stall him on that as long as we can," Frank said. "I'm just afraid he'll keep us at headquarters for hours. We don't have time for that."

"Nope," Joe said, checking his watch. "In fact, we'd better hurry over to the park if we want to catch Zack."

Within ten minutes Frank and Joe were back in the van, headed for the Bayport Skating Park. On the way over, Joe asked Frank how he was planning on checking out Torres's alibi.

"I'm thinking about when the mystery skater struck," Frank said. "The first time, Torres said he hadn't gotten into Bayport yet. The second time, he claimed to be practicing at the park. This last time, it may not have been the skater himself who put that goop in Zack's pool."

"So you're thinking it was the skater's accomplice," Joe said, pulling the van into the park's lot. He shut off the ignition and turned to his brother. "That's a tough one to check out. Why don't you watch me practice with Zack, and then we can both ask around the park afterward?"

Frank nodded. "Sounds good to me. There's plenty of time before the park closes. It's still only four," he said, checking his watch.

The crowds that had filled the Bayport Skating Park for the past few days had gotten even larger now that the big event was about to happen. As he and Frank walked through the park, Joe saw that there were more professional skaters than ever. He recognized many of them from their pictures in skateboarding magazines. Despite his preoccupation with the case, Joe felt a tingle of excitement at being around so many of the top skateboarding pros. With a firm hold on Zack's skateboard, Joe headed for the ramp where he'd arranged to meet Zack. The thrasher was waiting for the Hardys, his arm in a sling and a rueful grin on his face.

"The doctor said I should go straight home," Zack told Frank and Joe, "but I convinced my mom to drop me off here. I had to promise I wouldn't skate, though."

Joe strapped on his safety gear and got aboard Zack's skateboard. Zack quickly had Joe working out moves on a miniramp that was about half as tall as the big competition ramp. Joe was soon panting for breath and dripping sweat as Zack began relentlessly drilling him in various skating moves. But Joe was happy that the cord he had tied to the hook on the board wasn't slowing him down.

"Hey, stop a minute, Joe," Zack called. "I want to explain to you what you're doing wrong on your turns."

Joe stepped off the board and listened to Zack's instructions. "Maybe we should practice your turns in the tubeway," Zack suggested, "if it's free. That way you can concentrate on turning technique without worrying so much about getting high up on the vertical ramp."

"Sure, Zack. You're the coach," Joe said with a smile. He let out a big breath. It had already been a long day and he felt tired. But he knew it would be several more hours before he could rest.

Zack led Joe and Frank through the brightly lit park toward the tubeway, waving and talking to the other pro skaters. Joe saw that the tubeway wasn't in use, so he was free to practice on it. The air was filled with the sounds of skaters talking about the Thrashathon, the whizzing sound of wheels on concrete, and the pounding beat of rock music.

The pulsing rock rhythms helped Joe feel energetic as he began his practice run. He pushed off quickly and roared up one side of the concrete tubeway. He began performing aerial moves that sent him flying up over the side of the tubeway. Once Joe was airborne, he executed a 180-degree turn and then zoomed back down the tubeway again.

"That's good, Joe!" Zack shouted. "Stay loose at the top of the turn. Keep your knees flexed."

"You're getting to be a full-blown thrasher," Frank cried out.

Joe's series of ollies and turns had taken him to the other end of the tubeway, thirty feet away. With a roar, he pushed off and headed back toward Frank and Zack, where they sat at the top of the tube. The new speed and skill he had developed with Zack's help gave Joe a sense of exhilaration, and his earlier fatigue was replaced with a rush of energy. As he carved wide turns up the tube walls, his moves became rhythmic and effortless.

He practiced standing on his hands with the board balanced on his feet, and then on his shins. He came out of the position by grabbing the board with his left hand while supporting his weight with his right, and then, flipping down, landed with a loud whack on the board.

"Way to go!" Frank and Zack yelled in unison.

Joe was only fifteen feet away from Frank and Zack when he spotted a familiar black-clad arm stick up over the hedge along the right side of the tube.

"Joe! Look out!" Frank cried.

The mystery boarder, Joe thought, huddling down on his board. His heartbeat quickening, Joe swerved to avoid the guy. But just as Joe was cutting his move along the tubeway, a leather-gloved fist hurled a large handful of nuts, bolts, and ball bearings directly in Joe's path.

As the wheels of Joe's board collided with the

jumble of small metal parts, the board slammed to an abrupt stop. Joe instinctively grabbed for the bottom of the board, but it was no use. He lost his balance, and, in the next moment, felt himself falling sideways—ten feet to the bottom of the ramp!

11 Another Suspect

"Joe, watch out!" Frank cried, leaping off the top of the ramp. Zack moved as fast as he could but was hampered by his sling.

As Joe tried to get up on his hands and knees, Frank saw the mystery skater give a sharp tug on the nylon line that was attached to Zack's skateboard.

"He's trying to steal it," Frank yelled to Joe, hoping his shouts would make his brother realize what was happening.

Frank made his way down the curved wall, Zack behind him. In a flash, Frank saw the gleaming blade of a knife in the mystery skater's hand. The black-clad man reached down with a pocketknife and cut the cord that was attached to the skateboard.

Then the mystery skater scooped up the board and took off.

"Get him, Frank!" Zack shouted.

Frank ran along the bottom of the tubeway toward the mystery skater. I'm gaining on him, Frank thought.

Suddenly, the mystery skater turned around and hurled Zack's board at Frank's chest.

Caught off guard, Frank put out his arms and grabbed the board before it hit him. But the distraction gave the mystery boarder a bigger lead. Frank saw him exit the tubeway and turn left. Frank threw Zack's board down and raced after the skater. As he came out of the tubeway, Frank saw the skater mount a board waiting for him on the pavement, and he was off.

Frank heard two sets of footsteps running up behind him. He turned and saw that it was Zack and Joe, who was carrying Zack's board. With his one good arm, Zack pointed in the direction the skater had gone and shouted, "Hey, somebody stop that skater in black!"

The skaters and coaches at the nearby ramps turned in the direction of the shouts. Some of them watched the mystery skater zooming off through the park. But to the Hardys' frustration, no one made a move to stop him.

Frank looked on as the skater darted through the crowded park and shot under a wooden barricade like a rocket. Within seconds, he'd hopped the turnstiles at the end of the park and disappeared in the crowd.

"We lost him again," Frank said in frustration.

"At least he didn't get Zack's board," Joe said. He fingered the sheared nylon cord. "That was close, though."

"Are you guys okay?" Zack asked, a worried expression on his face.

Frank and Joe nodded.

"Hi, guys. Did I miss all the excitement?" a female voice called.

Frank looked over and saw Maggie Barnes coming toward them. "I saw some guy thrash out of here in a real big hurry," she said to Frank. "Who was he?"

"The same guy who's been making trouble for me all over town," Zack put in. "That skater is out to rip off my board, Maggie."

"Looks like you guys stopped him from stealing it," Maggie said with a smile.

"Just barely," Joe said grimly.

"Well, we've probably seen the last of him to-day," Frank said. "I don't think he'd be reckless enough to come back for another try."

"That means we may not have another chance before the Thrashathon to catch him," Zack said gloomily.

They all stood in silence for a few minutes. Then Joe's face lit up. "I just had a great idea," he said excitedly. "I'll go out tomorrow before the Thrashathon with Zack's board and let that skater steal it."

Maggie gave Frank a confused look. "What's your brother talking about?" she asked. "I thought the point was to stop the skater from stealing the board."

"Me, too," Frank said, turning to Joe. "Just what's on your mind?"

"Yeah, Joe," Zack said. "Why do you want him to steal the board? That's a crazy idea."

"It's not so crazy," Joe insisted. "As long as we use a decoy board with an electronic tracking device built into it."

Frank grinned at his brother. "Joe, you're a genius!"

Then Frank's expression turned serious. "The only problem with that is time. It might take too long to build a skateboard and tracker."

"No problem," Zack said. "Don't forget, I've got a fully equipped skateboard shop. I can build a copy of my board while you make the tracker."

"Great!" Joe said enthusiastically. "We've got enough electronic parts at home to construct a tracker. And we can put a microphone into it, too."

Frank nodded. "I've got a little condenser mike a friend of mine gave me a while ago. I was wondering what to use it for."

"This sounds like a perfect plan," Zack said. "If we use the high-tech approach, we'll definitely bag the mystery skater and his sidekick."

"Let's hope you're right," Frank said. "Can you get to work on the decoy board tonight?"

"No problem," Zack replied. "But one of you

will have to help me build it. My bad shoulder will make it tough since I can't really use both hands."

"I'll do it," Joe volunteered.

"Good. That way I can concentrate on building our bug," Frank said.

"That was a really rad suggestion," Zack said, patting Joe on the back. "You Hardys are definitely on the ball."

"I'll say," Maggie put in, obviously impressed. "Listen, Zack. I'm heading back to my hotel. Do you want a ride home?"

"That would be great. It'll give me a chance to fill you in on everything that's happened today."

Frank looked at Joe and said, "Before we go, we've got some unfinished business here at the park."

"I'll catch you in about an hour, Zack," Joe said. When Zack left with Maggie, Joe turned to his brother and said, "Torres . . . Something's been bothering me about that, Frank."

"What?" Frank asked his brother.

"The mystery skater's struck at least once since Zack made up with Torres," Joe pointed out. "At this point, what motive does Rick have for stealing Zack's board? And, besides, there's no evidence at all that it's Rick."

Frank was quiet for a few moments, thinking about what his brother had said. "You're right. Except that Torres could have been bluffing when he looked so happy about making things up with Zack. The fact is, when Zack stole those parts from

Alpine, Rick lost his job. The other fact is, Zack is Torres's biggest competitor in the Thrashathon. And the last fact is—"

"Barb Myers," Joe said, finishing the sentence for his brother. "And the lipstick on that cup."

"Right." Frank nodded. "It may be a long shot to go after Torres, but it's a chance we have to take."

"If Torres *was* in the park all day yesterday, as he claimed, then his name should be on some of the sign-up lists for the ramps," Joe said.

"Hey, you're right," Frank said. "Let's get going."

Frank led the way to the temporary office the Thrashathon staff had set up under a covered patio. Along the way, they passed by a U-shaped double half-pipe ramp where Danny Hayashi was practicing aerial turns. Chris Hall stood watching Hayashi, shouting instructions. A small cluster of young skateboarders stood behind Hall intently watching Hayashi. They suddenly cheered when the skater executed a spectacular twisting turn in the air. Joe heard shouts of "All right!" and "Radical thrashing, Danny!"

The Hardys stopped to watch for a moment, and as they stood there Frank spotted Barb Myers approaching the ramp. Rick Torres was with her, dressed in his Howling Wheels gear. He stood back, watching Hayashi and scowling. Unless I'm wrong, Frank thought, Rick looks a little worried about how good Hayashi's moves are.

While Hayashi kept up his double ollies, Frank

105

saw Barb Myers walk up to Chris Hall. The Howling Wheels owner didn't look happy. Myers exchanged a few words with Hall, which made the Scorpion Boards owner very angry. He said something to her that Frank couldn't hear, but whatever it was made Myers's face turn bright red. Frank edged closer to the couple, and before he knew it, Barb was shouting at Hall, her fists raised.

"You stink, Chris Hall!" Barb shouted, her dyed blond hair flying. "You're nothing but a low-down liar!"

At that moment, Rick must have noticed what was happening, because he ran up to Barb and put his arm around her.

Frank saw Hall give Torres a nasty smile. "Always coming to the rescue," Hall sneered. "You're out of your element, Torres," he added.

"What's this all about?" Frank heard Joe whisper to him. The crowd standing around Myers and Hall was silent, waiting to see what would happen. Barb just stood there, her face still bright red. Torres said something to her that seemed to calm her down, though, because Barb let him lead her away.

Chris Hall watched them leave, then announced to the crowd, "Just a little pre-Thrashathon jitters, folks. Nothing to worry about. Okay, Danny," he shouted to the thrasher. "Back to work."

After that, everyone began watching the skater again. Frank let out the long breath he'd been holding and tried to figure out what had just happened.

"Myers sure was angry," Joe said.

Frank nodded in agreement. "There's something going on between the two of them, that's for sure."

"What do you think it is?" Joe asked.

"I don't know," Frank said. "But I'll bet you anything Rick Torres could explain it to us." Frank watched Torres lead Barb over to the Howling Wheels tent. Soon, the two of them were packing up their gear. Frank realized that the Thrashathon's staff was also about to close down for the night.

"It looks as though we'll have to wait to talk to him," Frank said. "Come on, let's check out those sign-up sheets before the staff goes home."

When Frank and Joe got to the patio, Frank saw a row of tables manned by teenagers who were wearing Thrashathon T-shirts. One of the tables had a card taped to it marked Pro Skater Sign-Up.

"Leave this to me," Frank told his brother as he walked over to the table.

"Hi," Frank said to a blond girl sitting behind the table.

"Hello. Can I help you?" the girl replied, looking up from her clipboard.

"I hope so," Frank said with a smile. "I want to see if a friend of mine from out of town took in the practice sessions yesterday. I waited to see him all day today, but he never showed up. So I want to know if he was here before."

"I can check the sign-up lists for the ramps," the girl suggested. "That should tell you."

"You look busy," Frank said sympathetically. "If you give me that list, I can look it up myself."

"I am pretty busy," the girl said with a smile. "I have to finish a bunch of paperwork before I can pack up for the night." She searched through the pile of papers on the table and pulled out a different clipboard. "Here you go," she said, handing it to Frank.

Frank turned away from the table and quickly riffled through the papers on the clipboard. He saw that it contained sign-up lists for all the ramps. As he scanned the sheets, looking for the list from the day before, Joe came up to him.

"If Torres was telling the truth, then his name will be on yesterday's lists from noon to around three in the afternoon," Joe said, recalling when the mystery skater had struck.

"Let's see," Frank said, flipping through the pages. He searched through several sheets but couldn't find the list for the day before. "That's funny," he said.

"What is?" Joe asked, leaning over Frank's shoulder.

"The list that would have the practice sign-ups from yesterday is missing," he said. "Excuse me," Frank said, turning back to the table where the blond girl was starting to pack up her notebooks and clipboards. "The sign-up sheet from yesterday is missing," he told her. "Would you happen to know where it is?"

The girl made a face as Frank handed her the clipboard. She riffled through the sheets and said, "That's very strange. I know I had it at the end of the day yesterday, but now it's gone. Sorry," she added. "I can't help you out."

Frank shrugged. "That's okay. I guess I'll just have to hope he shows up tomorrow. The guy's a flake sometimes."

The girl smiled. "That's the way it is with thrashers," she said. "Even in professional competitions, they can have a hard time sticking to schedules."

"Yeah. Thanks," Frank said as he and Joe walked away from the table.

"Well, there goes that lead," Joe said. He looked at his watch. "We should head over to Zack's now," Joe said. "It's going to take us a while to build that board."

Frank ran his hands through his hair and watched as the park started to empty after the day's events. "You're right," he said.

"Hey," Joe put in, "don't worry. Our decoy board is going to catch the skater—whoever he is!"

Frank wished he could be as enthusiastic as Joe. So far, most of their leads had been total dead ends.

"I'll drop you off at Zack's," Frank told Joe. "Then I'll head home, check on the fingerprint test, and pick up the electronics gear for the decoy."

Joe nodded, and the two Hardys headed out of the park. Within fifteen minutes, Frank and Joe were pulling up in front of Zack's house. There was a sound of power tools coming from the garage, so Frank headed in that direction, assuming Zack was already at work.

When he got to the garage, Frank was startled at what greeted him. Rick Torres was standing at Zack's shoulder, watching him work, giving him instructions.

As soon as Joe appeared by Frank's side, the younger Hardy shouted, "Hey, Zack!"

Zack and Rick both turned to face the Hardys. "Rick stopped by. He's helping me out," Zack said. "I told him about our plan."

Frank's heart sank in his stomach. If Torres was the mystery skater, their decoy plan was shot now. "That's great," Frank said weakly, forcing a smile in Rick's direction.

"And he's got some news, too," Zack said. "Tell them, Rick."

Torres switched off the drill he was holding and cleared his throat. "It's about Barb Myers," he said.

"What about Myers?" Joe asked enthusiastically.

Frank saw Rick pause a moment and bite on his lip, obviously deciding whether or not to go ahead with what he was about to say.

"Tell them, Rick," Zack urged.

Rick took a deep breath. "Okay. Unless I'm wrong, I think Barb Myers is the one who's after Zack's board. I think she's the person behind the mystery skater!"

12 A Clever Trap

"Barb Myers!" Joe said, letting the news sink in. "You really think she could be the one trying to steal your board?" he asked Zack.

"That's why Rick came by," Zack said. He set his drill down and gestured with his good arm. "Tell them, Rick."

The Hardys listened as Rick relayed his story. "When I told Barb about how Zack had stolen those parts from Alpine, she was convinced that Zack had used them to build a souped-up skateboard. She always thought there was something special about Zack's board. I told her I didn't know anything about it, that Zack and I were friends again, and that Zack was going to get me my job back."

"And I will," Zack promised.

"And I still believe you, man," Rick said. "Anyway," he went on, "Barb told me I was a fool to trust Zack. She tried to poison me against you," he confessed to Zack. "Then she started asking me all sorts of questions about Zack's board. She wanted me to help her get her hands on it."

"But did Barb have someone else try to steal it?" Frank asked.

Torres shook his head. "Nope. At least she didn't mention it. But I wouldn't put it past her. She's really got it in for you, Zack, ever since you quit Howling Wheels."

Zack hung his head. "I know, I know. Maybe it was a stupid thing to do, but I wanted to be a free agent."

"Have you seen Barb talking to any skaters lately?" Joe asked. "Anyone she might have hired to help her steal Zack's board?"

Rick thought for a minute. "Barb's always trying to recruit guys for her team. I've seen her with Danny Hayashi a lot in the past few days, but I thought that was to get at Chris Hall."

Joe remembered the argument he'd seen between Hall and Myers that afternoon at the skating park. "What's going on between Barb and Chris, anyway?" he asked Rick.

"You got me," Torres said. "Every time I ask her about it, she just clams up. That guy really gets to her, though."

"I just had an idea," Frank said. He went to sit on the beat-up couch and rested his elbows on his knees. "What if Barb knows about your deal with Hall and wants to get in on it? She already suspects you've got a radical board. Maybe she's working it both ways."

"Huh?" Joe asked, giving his brother a confused look and trying to follow Frank's reasoning. "What do you mean by 'both ways'?"

Frank spelled it out. "One: She tries to steal Zack's board. Since that hasn't been working out for her, she tries the other option: getting in on Zack's deal with Chris. That could have been what they were arguing about at the park earlier."

"Wait a minute," Torres said, holding his hands out palms up. "Would you care to explain what this is all about? What deal with Chris?"

Joe began to feel really uncomfortable. He knew Zack hadn't told Rick yet about his deal with Scorpion Boards. Now Frank had accidentally spilled the beans.

"Uh, I think that's for Zack to explain," Joe said, giving Frank a look that told him not to reveal anything more until Zack had a chance to tell his friend about the deal.

Zack fumbled for a moment, then went on to explain to Rick all about his agreement with Chris Hall. "I wanted to tell you," Zack finished. "But nothing is finalized until Chris sees how my board performs in competition. After the Thrashathon we're supposed to sit down and hash out the details."

Torres sank into the armchair next to the sofa.

113

"That just blows me away," he said. "I can't believe you didn't tell me."

"Well, I have some other deals on the back burner," Zack said. "Like I said, nothing is definite yet."

"Zack kind of wanted to surprise you," Joe said, putting in a good word for his friend. "He's going to split the profits with you. Aren't you, Zack?"

The thrasher nodded. "Fifty-fifty."

Rick looked at Zack between narrowed eyes, obviously trying to decide if he should trust him. "Fifty-fifty?" he asked suspiciously.

"For sure," Zack said. "When a deal comes through, you won't even need to go back to Alpine Bikes."

Finally, Torres started to become convinced. He stood up again, walked over to Zack, and reached out to shake his hand. Zack laughed and held out his good arm. He pumped Rick's hand and said, "Partners?"

"Partners," Torres said.

"I hate to break this up," Joe said, looking at his watch, "but we're running out of time, and that board is a long way from being done."

Zack laughed. "Let's get to it."

While Zack and Rick went back to working on the board, Joe sat down next to Frank on the couch. "You really think it's Barb?" he asked his brother.

"She's got the motive," Frank said slowly. "She's not the type to think twice about getting even with

114

Zack. And from that argument we overheard, she seems to have a real grudge against Hall, too. He might have promised her he'd let her in on the deal, and then backed out."

Joe sighed. "We'll know a lot more when the skater steals the decoy board," he said. "With some luck, whoever it is will lead us back to Barb."

"*If* the skater steals the board," Frank said. "I just hope it works."

"It will," Joe said emphatically. "It has to. Now why don't you head home to get the electronic gear while I help Zack and Rick put together the board?"

"Sounds good," Frank said. "I can check the report on those fingerprints while I'm home."

"Cool," Joe said. "Maybe there will be a lead there."

Frank took off, and Joe went to help Rick and Zack work on putting together an exact replica of Zack's custom board. Fortunately Zack had plenty of skateboarding stickers to plaster all over the decoy board to make it look just like his custom board. Zack instructed Joe to carve a small cavity in the wooden deck. It was just big enough to house the tracker and microphone that Frank would make. Then Torres drilled holes into the bottom of the board for the trucks. By the time they were done, Frank came back with the electronics parts.

From the worried expression on Frank's face, Joe guessed the results of the fingerprinting test weren't much help. "No luck, huh?" he asked Frank as the older Hardy set down a box full of parts, wires, and tools.

"Nope," Frank said. "Neither set of prints turned up a match. Whoever's been watching that house doesn't have a record—that's why the computer didn't find a match."

Joe scratched his head. "I still think the lipstick on that cup was Barb's. From what Rick said, I'll bet Barb has been spying on Zack in order to get her hands on his board."

"You could be right," Frank said as he removed the parts from the box. "But until we catch her, there's no proof."

Joe helped his brother set up the equipment at one end of Zack's workbench. Frank had brought along a simple battery-powered transmitter that would serve as the tracker. Along with the transmitter, Frank quickly rigged a receiver by modifying an old shortwave radio that had been gathering dust in a closet at the Hardy home.

With Zack and Rick working on the board, and Frank and Joe putting together the electronics, the time passed quickly. They only stopped working long enough to wolf down the tray of sandwiches and sodas Mrs. Michaels brought out to Zack's shop shortly before ten. When the decoy and bug were finally in place, it was almost midnight. Joe watched as Frank put the finishing touches on the microphone, set it inside the board, and pasted the hole over with a long skateboarding sticker.

"That ought to hold it," Frank said, stifling a yawn.

"One final thing," Zack said, taking the board from Frank. He found a piece of coarse sandpaper and rubbed it vigorously over the board, top and bottom. "This will make it look as if it's been in action for a while."

"That should do it," Joe said. "Now I think we should make sure it works." He took the board and put it down on the ground and popped a wheelie. "I'll take it for a spin. See if you can follow."

With that, Joe skated out of Zack's garage and onto the street. He shot along the nearly empty street, took a corner with his knees bent and popped the board around when he got to the end of the block. When he got back in front of Zack's house, he asked, "Okay, where'd I go?"

Zack smiled and held out the transmitter. "Not very far."

"Just halfway around the block, I'd say," Frank said.

"All right!" Joe cried. "It works."

Rick stretched his arms over his head and yawned. "It's a good thing, too," he said, "because I'm exhausted."

"Me, too," Zack said, rubbing his injured shoulder. "It's been a long day. I think we should call it a night. I'm about ready to drop."

Joe and Frank made plans to meet at Zack's house the next morning. Then they took Rick back to his hotel and headed for home. When Joe's head hit the pillow, he fell asleep instantly, dreaming about finally catching the mystery skater on their deluxe custom decoy skateboard.

The next morning Joe awoke early, too excited to sleep anymore. He climbed out of bed and stretched his body, which was stiff from his skateboarding workout the night before. As he headed for the bathroom for a shower, he wondered what he was more excited about: bagging the mystery skater or competing in his first skateboarding competition.

Frank was up a few minutes after Joe. After a quick breakfast of juice and fruit, they piled in the van and headed for Zack's house. When they got there, Zack was up and ready to go.

At ten after seven, the three of them headed outside. Joe pushed off down the street on the decoy skateboard.

Frank manned the tracker's receiver in the back of the van while Zack drove. Frank had instructed Zack to hang back at least a block behind Joe. Joe practiced doing wheelies and popping ollies over curbs as he rode through the quiet streets around Zack's house.

Joe kept an eye on the street as first one, then two hours passed without the mystery skater appearing. He was almost beginning to wonder if the skater was going to appear at all. Then, as Joe swerved to avoid a line of cars parked along the curb of one street, a dark object darted out from between two cars.

The mystery skater! Joe thought.

Suddenly, the black-clad boarder reached out and knocked Joe from the skateboard.

"Oof!" As Joe fell he tucked himself into a ball and then rolled toward the edge of the street. Catching his breath on the curb, he watched the skater take off like a rocket on the decoy board. Just then, Zack swerved up to him in the van with a squeal of tires.

"Let's go!" Zack cried, moving over to the passenger seat to let Joe drive.

Joe bounded into the van, and the chase was on!

13 Tracking a Thrasher

Joe threw the van into gear and roared off after the mystery skater.

"Don't get too close to him," Frank cautioned from the back of the van. "We don't want him to know he's being followed."

Joe eased up on the gas. Frank kept his eyes on the skater, making sure that he hadn't spotted the Hardys' van.

"How's our signal?" Joe asked.

"Loud and clear," Frank said proudly. "This thing works great!"

In his earphones, Frank could hear the slow, regular beeps of the track's sign suddenly beginning to beep faster as the skater moved farther up the street.

"Don't follow him straight down Bank Street," Frank instructed. "Take a left onto Flower Street. It parallels Bank, and we can track him without risking being seen."

Joe made a turn. Frank followed the signals for several blocks.

"He's not moving very fast," Frank told Joe and Zack. "I don't think he knows we're following him."

"Perfect," Joe said. "This is going just like we planned."

They drove on in silence for another few blocks. The only sound inside the car was the regular high-pitched pinging sound of the tracker. Suddenly there was a Do Not Enter sign directly in their path.

"Frank, we've got trouble," Joe called out over his shoulder. "Flower Street changes to a one-way street on the next block."

"Turn left at the intersection and go over two streets so we can keep paralleling the skater's course," Frank suggested.

"Right," Joe replied.

Joe stopped at the intersection, then turned left onto the cross street. The van was about halfway down the block when Frank realized that the signal was changing. "He's doubling back toward us!" Frank called out.

A moment later, Frank spotted the mystery skater on the left side of the street, coming straight toward the van. The skater must have seen them, because

121

he put on a burst of speed and zoomed right past.

"Hang on!" Joe said tensely as he slammed on the brakes. He quickly turned into a driveway, then backed out so he could reverse his direction.

"I see him," Zack cried. "He's cutting down the one-way street."

"We can't follow him," Joe said. "Do you remember how far Flower Street runs one way?"

"Yeah," Frank replied. "It runs six blocks as a one-way street and ends up in the downtown area."

"What are we going to do? He's going to get away," Zack said anxiously.

"Relax, Zack. My receiver can pick up a signal from at least a mile away. And I've still got a strong signal," Frank told him.

"We're not losing him if I have anything to say about it," Joe said with determination.

He sped past the one-way street the skater had taken and turned onto the next street to keep running parallel to the skater's path.

"It looks as though he's staying on the same street," Frank commented. "We may have a chance of catching up to him when he hits Main Street."

"Yeah, if all the traffic on Main Street doesn't hit us first," Joe muttered.

Frank looked out the windshield and saw that they were heading down a street lined with houses. He saw several groups of kids playing on the sidewalk and told Joe to slow down just in case one of the children darted out into the street. In the meantime, he kept his ears peeled to the signal coming through the phones. After keeping up with the skater for a few more blocks, Frank realized that the signal was starting to fade.

"We're losing him," Frank said urgently. "Can't you go any faster?"

"Not without exceeding the speed limit," Joe replied. "I thought you said the tracker had a range of a mile."

"It does," Frank said, barely keeping the frustration out of his voice. "I don't understand it. Wait a minute!" he cried suddenly. "I know why it's breaking up. The skater must be going into an area where there's more metal in the buildings. That could interfere with the signal."

"Can't you do anything?" Zack asked.

"Not unless we can get closer to him," Frank replied. "I think he's heading down toward Marlborough Street, which runs parallel to Main Street."

"Then maybe we can still get him," Joe said. "There's a big construction site near there. We could cut across it."

"It's chancy, but we'll have to risk it," Frank said. "Otherwise, he'll get away."

"Let's do it, guys!" Zack urged.

Joe pressed down the accelerator. The crowded residential neighborhoods gave way to more sparsely populated streets lined with warehouses and storefronts.

Joe hung a tight left turn, and suddenly there was

a construction site spread out along the block ahead. As Joe drove along the site, Zack pointed to a swiftly moving black figure on the sidewalk ahead of them.

"There he is!" Zack shouted. "He's cutting through the construction site!"

Joe steered the van halfway down the block until he came to an opening in the chain-link fencing around the site.

"Go for it!" Frank shouted.

Joe didn't hesitate. He plowed the van through the fence and followed the skater despite the shouts from startled construction workers.

"How's the signal, Frank?" Joe asked.

"It's breaking up! There's too much metal in the buildings here," Frank said, growing frustrated.

"Can you see him, Joe?" Zack asked, craning his neck toward the windshield.

"No, there's too much stuff in the way," Joe shouted back.

Joe continued down the dirt road next to the site. Frank held his breath as Joe swerved to avoid colliding with a bulldozer. His ears still intent on the skater's signal, Frank kept his eyes peeled for a sign of the skater. Finally, he saw a fleeting glimpse of the mystery skater between the steel-girdered skeletons of two unfinished buildings.

"I see him!" Frank cried out. "He's almost at the other side of the site." The beeps in Frank's earphones started to get fainter. "The signal's fading!" he yelled. "It's now or never."

With the black-clad skater in view, Joe increased his speed. But the mystery skater reached the sidewalk on the other side of the construction site, popped an ollie over the curb, and carved a sharp right turn.

Frank lost sight of the skater after that. The signal in his earphones blipped once and then disappeared. "That's it, guys," he announced grimly. "I've just lost the signal."

"What happened?" Zack asked. "I thought you'd be able to track him once we were away from all that metal."

"He could have gone beneath a traffic underpass with a lot of steel girders in it," Joe said. "There's one in the next block."

"Let's keep going, anyway," Frank urged. "Maybe I can pick up the signal again."

"Hey, guys," Zack asked suddenly. "Are we anywhere near the Bayport Arms Hotel?"

"I think we're about two blocks from there," Frank said. "Why?"

"Maggie's staying there, and she said a lot of skaters from the Thrashathon are registered, too," Zack said excitedly.

"All right, Zack!" Joe and Frank shouted in unison.

Joe plowed through an underpass and made his way to the Bayport Arms. There was a parking space directly in front of the hotel, and Joe steered the van into it.

"I need you both to be very quiet for a minute,"

Frank cautioned. "I'm going to try and pick up something on the mike inside the board."

While Joe and Zack watched intently, Frank carefully tuned the receiver to the microphone's frequency. At first there was only static coming from the small speaker on the receiver. Then Frank made a minor adjustment, and they all heard what sounded like footsteps and someone breathing hard.

The sounds went on for several minutes.

"It sounds like he's climbing stairs," Zack whispered.

"Shh," Frank said.

From the corner of his eye, Joe saw Frank flick on a small tape recorder that was patched into a microphone lead on the receiver.

"Way to go, Frank," Joe whispered.

Frank flashed Joe a smile, then motioned for him to be quiet.

Joe heard the sound of someone beating loudly on a door.

"Who is it?" a muffled voice called.

"It's me—Danny. I got the board. Open up!"

Frank looked up at Zack and Joe. The identity of their mystery skater wasn't a mystery anymore.

"Danny Hayashi!" Zack exclaimed.

14 A Dirty Maneuver

"Wow!" Zack's eyes grew wide with surprise. "Danny Hayashi's the one who's been after my board this whole time! What a rat."

Frank motioned for Zack to be quiet. From the noises he heard coming from the bug, he figured Danny was walking into the hotel room. He tried to make out the voice of the person Danny was talking to, but whoever it was spoke too softly.

"It's impossible to tell who he's talking to," Frank said under his breath.

"You can't even tell if it's a man or a woman," Joe said, leaning toward the speaker. "The sounds are too muffled."

Just then, a series of loud thumping and knocking noises came through the speaker. Frank heard

Danny's voice cry, "Hey! What's this on the bottom?"

Frank looked up at Joe. Zack bit on his lip. All three of them knew what was about to happen.

"This isn't Zack's board!" Danny cried. "We've been duped."

Loud scraping noises came through the speaker, then a pop.

"He's found the bug," Frank whispered.

Joe covered his face with his hands. "Great, just great," he said.

"There are wires in here . . ." came Danny's voice. "And a microphone. We've been bugged!"

Frank heard a loud smashing sound, and then the receiver went totally dead.

"There goes that plan," Frank said in a disgusted voice as he turned off the receiver.

"But the important thing is that we taped Hayashi talking about ripping off Zack's board," Joe pointed out.

"That's true," Frank said, nodding. "Unfortunately, we still don't know who put Hayashi up to it."

The three boys were silent for several minutes. Zack bit on a fingernail and tapped his foot with impatience. "All I know," he said, "is that the Thrashathon starts in an hour and we still don't know who's really after my board."

"And I have to get to the park to sign up," Joe put in, "or else I lose my spot in the competition."

"I know, I know," Frank said in frustration. "I

thought this would work." He threw the earphones down and took a deep breath. "Something has to give."

"One thing's for sure," Joe said. "We're not getting anywhere sitting here." He paused for a moment. "Maybe you should stake out the hotel, Frank. See who Hayashi leaves with. Zack and I can head over to the park."

Frank thought about Joe's suggestion. "That's not a bad idea, except that in the time I'm gone to take you to the park, Hayashi could leave the hotel. Then the trail would be ice-cold all over again."

"So what should we do?" Joe asked, his voice rising.

"Hayashi's working for someone, right?" Frank said, thinking out loud. "All we have to do is figure out who that could be."

Zack spoke up. "Rick said he saw Barb talking to Danny a lot lately, remember?"

"That's right!" Frank cried. "But how do we nail her? It's still only a suspicion."

"There's only one reason Barb would try to steal the board—maybe she can't afford to pay Zack for the design," Joe put in.

"How can we find out if that's true?" Zack asked. "Barb's not going to volunteer the information that she's broke."

"No," Frank said. He had to think—fast. They were running out of time. "But we could do some fast research into Howling Wheels." Frank looked at his watch. "Let's go, Joe," he said.

"Where to?" Joe asked.

"I'll drop you guys off at the skating park and then zoom over to the library," Frank said. He got out of the van and went around to the driver's side.

"The library?" Joe said, climbing into the back of the van.

Frank started up the van. "I want to do some research on Howling Wheels. If Barb's company is in trouble, it'll show up on the financial records."

Zack looked at Frank. "Is there time?" he asked.

"I hope so," Frank said, pulling out into traffic.

Frank first stopped at Zack's house to pick up the thrasher's board. Then he dropped Joe and Zack off at the skating park. Finally, Frank headed to the Bayport Public Library. As he was pulling into the parking lot, he realized he'd better call Con Riley to update him on their progress. He picked up the van's cellular phone and punched in Con Riley's office number. Within a few minutes, Frank had explained to Riley about the decoy board and Danny Hayashi.

"We might need an assist at the park later," Frank said. "But I want Hayashi to lead us to his accomplice, so I don't want to nab him yet."

"I've got some officers working crowd control at the skating park," Riley said. "I'll put them on alert and tell them to keep an eye on Hayashi. If he does anything sneaky, we'll be tailing him."

"Thanks, Con," Frank said, hanging up.

Frank rushed into the library and headed straight for the periodicals desk. Mrs. Fichelli, the dark-haired librarian, smiled broadly when she saw Frank approaching.

"Hello," she said cheerily. "What brings you here? Working on a case?"

"I sure am," Frank replied. "And I hope you can help me out. Where can I find financial information on specific companies?" Frank asked her.

"There's a guide to American businesses on the shelves behind you," she answered. "The companies are listed alphabetically by the products they make."

Frank thanked her. Then he headed over to the shelf she had pointed out. Frank pulled out the S volume and quickly turned to the page in the book dealing with skateboarding companies.

Frank ran his finger down the page until he came to a listing for Howling Wheels. All the financial information was there, including a list of people who had invested in the company. Barb Myers's name appeared, along with the number of stocks she owned. Frank searched for some sign that the company was in trouble, but if anything, Howling Wheels appeared to be making more of a profit than Barb had let on to Zack.

"For someone who doesn't pay her skaters," Frank said to himself, "she sure does keep a lot of money."

Frank sat down in a nearby armchair with the

book in his lap. He went back over the numbers, but it all added up to one thing: Howling Wheels was in fine financial shape. Barb could easily afford to pay Zack for his design if she wanted to. That fact didn't rule out the possibility that Barb might have been trying to steal Zack's board, though.

Drumming his fingers on the book, Frank tried to think up another angle—something that would prove Barb was after Zack's board. His eyes roamed the page that listed other skateboarding companies, some of whose names he recognized: Zebra Boards, Scorpion Boards—Chris Hall's company. Frank skimmed through the information on Scorpion, when some unsettling figures caught his eye.

The company had been operating at a loss for well over two years. Frank knew that was nothing new, since smaller companies sometimes took a while to make a profit. But Scorpion had also been borrowing heavily in the past six months. That wasn't a good sign for Zack, Frank thought. If Scorpion didn't have the money to buy the thrasher's design, Chris Hall wouldn't be able to produce and manufacture the boards—unless Hall borrowed even more money. Then Frank saw something even more upsetting: Scorpion was the target of several lawsuits, one of them from a former stockholder named Evan Hall. The information about the lawsuit even said that Evan was Chris Hall's own brother.

Frank shut the book, letting the news sink in.

From all the facts he'd just read, Frank began to suspect that Chris Hall wasn't exactly a trustworthy businessman. He was heavily in debt, and his own brother had sued him. Frank decided to track down Evan Hall to see if Chris's brother could shed some light on just what was going on with Scorpion's finances.

Frank found a pay phone near the library exit. The report on Scorpion listed Evan Hall as living in Boston. Frank sat down in the booth and dialed Massachusetts information, then asked the operator for Boston and the number of Evan Hall. There were three Evan Halls listed. The first two Frank reached had never heard of Scorpion Boards. He dialed the third Evan Hall. This has to be the right one, he thought.

"Mr. Evan Hall?" Frank asked when he heard a gruff voice say hello on the other end of the phone.

"Yes. Who wants to know?" the voice asked suspiciously.

"My name's Hardy, Mr. Hall," Frank said. "I'm a detective doing some research into your brother's company, Scorpion Boards."

"Scorpion Boards," Hall snarled. "Boy, could I give you an earful about that company."

"Go ahead, Mr. Hall, I'm listening," Frank said, trying to keep the excitement out of his voice.

"My brother is ripping off his stockholders by skimming profits," Hall said. "He's running his company into the ground."

"Are you trying to tell me Scorpion Boards is in serious trouble?" Frank asked.

Hall laughed bitterly. "Mister, I know for a fact that the only thing keeping that company afloat now is the money Chris borrowed from loan sharks. He's desperate for money, and he'll do anything to get it! Lie, cheat, or steal. Anything!"

15 The Bayport Thrashathon

"Is there anything else you can tell me about Scorpion Boards, Mr. Hall?" Frank pressed. He was anxious to learn everything he could before Hall got off the line.

"That's all, I guess," Evan Hall replied. "My brother's greed has drained Scorpion Boards dry. That company is going under soon, and I can't wait to see it happen."

"A report I read said you're suing your brother," Frank said. "Exactly what is the lawsuit about?" he asked.

There was a long pause at the other end. "My lawyer says not to discuss the details," Hall said, avoiding the question. "I can only tell you that the case has to do with money he owes me. I doubt I'll ever see it, but even if the case only proves my brother is a crook, I'll be happy."

"I understand," Frank said, more than a little surprised at just how much Evan Hall disliked his brother. Whatever had happened between them was enough to make Evan Hall want to ruin Chris. That was pretty strong stuff. "Thank you for your time. I'm sure this information will help my investigation quite a bit."

"Hey," Hall said. "Just what are you investigating, anyway? What's my brother done now?"

Frank thought quickly. "I'm afraid that information is confidential," he said. "I can't discuss anything until we actually have a case against Mr. Hall."

"I see," Evan said. "Well, I hate to say it, because he is my brother and all, but Chris has made some very bad decisions with his company. He's going to see that eventually he has to suffer the consequences."

Frank quickly thanked Hall for his time and hung up. He rushed from the library, almost forgetting to return the volume he was holding to the periodical room. Frank put the book back and hurried to the parking lot. He couldn't wait to tell Joe what he'd just learned.

While Frank raced over to the skating park, he started putting the pieces together. Obviously, Hall's company was in enough trouble that it seemed unlikely Chris would be able to pay Zack for his design.

"And obviously," Frank said out loud, "Chris Hall thought of another way to get his hands on the board: have Danny Hayashi steal it."

Frank darted the van through an intersection, just catching the light before it turned yellow. He had to get to the park before Hayashi tried to steal Zack's board again. If Danny got away with it, Frank and Joe would have a hard time tracing the theft back to Chris Hall. The information Frank had learned from Evan Hall didn't *prove* Chris Hall tried to steal Zack's skateboard. But all the evidence pointed to the fact that Hall had a strong motive for wanting to steal it.

Driving quickly, Frank arrived at the skating park within ten minutes. After parking the van, Frank hurried inside the park and over to the judge's table to find out where Joe was competing.

He was about to ask one of the judges how he might find his brother when the speakers over his head crackled. An announcer's booming voice said that the next two competitors at that ramp would be Danny Hayashi and Joe Hardy.

Frank pushed through the crowd and breathlessly arrived at the competition ramp just as Danny Hayashi was stepping onto his board.

Zack was standing by, giving Joe last minute instructions. Joe readjusted his safety helmet and spotted his brother.

"Hey, Frank," Zack called out. "What's up?"

"Did you learn anything?" Joe asked, skating up closer to Frank. "Danny's had his eye on me ever since we got here."

Frank looked over and saw Danny perform his first move, a rapid climb up the wall of the ramp that climaxed in a spectacular one-handed handstand on the lip of the ramp.

"Have you seen Chris?" Frank asked Joe and Zack, searching the crowd for some sign of the Scorpion Board's owner.

"Chris?" Zack asked, a confused expression on his face. "Why do you want to find Chris?"

"Because I think he's the one who got Danny to try to steal your board," Frank announced.

Zack's face dropped, and Joe's eyes went wide with surprise. Frank quickly explained what he'd learned from Evan Hall, and gave Joe his theories about how Chris Hall didn't have the money to pay Zack for his design.

"So you think he's been trying to steal my board instead?" Zack said, keeping his voice low. "Wow!"

Just then Danny finished his moves, and the crowd broke out in a round of applause. A moment later the announcer called out Joe's name.

"What should I do?" Joe asked. "We have to catch Hall, but I'm up next."

"You go ahead," Frank told his brother. "I'll scout the crowd and see if I can find Hall."

Frank waited a minute while his brother took his place on the competition ramp. Joe was obviously

138

nervous, and Frank wanted to make sure that he started out all right.

"Can he do it?" Frank asked Zack.

Zack nodded confidently. "Joe's a good thrasher. He may not beat Danny, but he'll still make my board look good." Zack paused. "According to the rules of elimination competition," he quickly explained, "Joe is supposed to duplicate Hayashi's move or add another maneuver to it."

Frank saw his brother zoom up the wall of the ramp wearing a determined expression. Joe executed a one-handed handstand, then did a complete flip in the air. Joe came back down the wall wearing a triumphant grin.

Frank was about to leave and look for Hall when he saw Hayashi, who was standing near the left side of the ramp, kick his board right out into Joe's path.

With a feeling of helplessness, Frank realized there was no way for Joe to avoid it. He winced as he saw Joe lose his footing on his board and slam into the bottom of the half-pipe.

Hayashi's dirty trick caused an immediate commotion in the judges' box. Several judges stood up from their seats wearing expressions that ranged from surprise to outrage.

The crowd suddenly erupted in loud boos and jeers. Hayashi threw up his hands and tried to pretend it was an accident, but the crowd wasn't buying it. Many of the spectators hurled wadded-up soda cups and Thrashathon programs at Hayashi.

"Hey, I'm sorry," Hayashi said quickly as he

ducked the rain of trash. "My board got away from me. It was an accident, really."

"Yeah, right," Zack said, glaring in Danny's direction.

Frank watched angrily as Hayashi went over to Joe and held out a hand to help him up. Joe slapped it away and tried to stagger upright. As he did, Joe fell backward. Danny took advantage of Joe's fall to reach out and grab Zack's board.

Frank realized with a shock what Danny was planning. Hayashi had the board in his hand and was scanning the crowd for an escape. The skater was about to get away with Zack's board!

Frank quickly pushed his way through the people. When he got beyond the crowd, he saw that Rick Torres was already helping Joe to his feet.

Frank kept his eyes on Danny to make sure the thrasher didn't make a run for it. At that moment, Torres turned to Danny and said something that Frank couldn't hear. Hayashi dropped the board, drew back his fist, and hit Torres with a blow to the jaw that knocked him to the ground.

Frank and Zack elbowed their way to the base of the ramp. They were joined by several other competitors and three judges from the Thrashathon.

"What do you think you're doing?" an angry judge snapped at Hayashi. "This is a competition, not a boxing ring."

"Hayashi was trying to take me out of the competition," Joe replied, scooping up Zack's board.

Torres stood up, rubbing his jaw. "He kicked his

board right out in front of Joe," Torres told the judges. "It looked deliberate from where I was standing. Joe could have broken his neck!"

"I know," one of the judges said. "We saw the whole thing." He turned to the crowd and announced, "Ladies and gentlemen, we have a temporary delay in the competition. Danny Hayashi has just been eliminated for endangering another skater, and we need to reschedule some of the events."

Frank saw Hayashi follow the judges and heard him try to talk them into reinstating him, but they wouldn't change their ruling.

"Are you all right, Joe?" Frank asked.

Joe nodded. "I've got a few bruises, but I can still compete."

"Good," Frank said. "You stay here and keep an eye on Hayashi. Make sure he doesn't take off. I'm going to find Chris Hall."

At that moment, Frank spotted Maggie Barnes. "Hey, Maggie!" Frank shouted. "Have you seen Chris Hall?"

"I think you'll find him over in the parking lot that's reserved for visiting pros," Maggie replied. "What's going on, anyway?" she asked, a curious expression on her face.

"Zack can explain everything," Frank said, taking off at a run and leaving Maggie Barnes standing there with her mouth open.

"Don't you want me to come with you?" Joe called out.

Frank turned and yelled back to Joe over his

141

shoulder, "Find a police officer and have Hayashi arrested. Now that he's been eliminated, he may try to escape. I'll take care of Hall myself."

Without wasting another second, Frank rushed to the pro skaters' parking lot. When he got there, Frank made his way around the parked cars, looking around for any sign of Hall. The Scorpion Board's owner wasn't there, but Frank found a big pickup truck with the company's logo painted on the door.

Frank peered into the truck's interior, but there was nothing suspicious inside. He went around to the back of the truck, which was covered with a sliding panel that was locked. Frank quickly took his lock-pick kit from his wallet and went to work. After a few moments, he heard the cover pop open.

Frank pulled the lid open, and his eyes widened when he saw what was inside the truck's bed. The mystery skater's black costume and black skateboard were carelessly shoved in beside the spare tire. Frank also saw a plastic bucket of silicone lubricant.

A small, tightly wrapped bundle caught his eye, and he pulled it out of the truck. When he unwrapped it, he saw that it was a compact and remarkably complete set of burglar tools.

"Anything interesting in there?" a voice behind him with a strong Boston accent suddenly asked.

As Frank turned to face the speaker, he felt a fist punch him hard in the side. Stunned by the pain, he fell to his knees, clutching his side. As he staggered to his feet he heard Hall's truck roar to life.

"Hall!" Frank shouted, knowing it was too late. With a frustrated sigh, Frank watched the truck zoom toward the parking lot exit.

16 Nailing a Thief

Shaking off the pain, Frank ran to the parking lot attendant's booth. "I've got to stop that truck. Can you let me call one of the officers?"

"Sure," the attendant replied. "Here's my walkie-talkie." He handed him the device and told him which buttons to use.

Frank took it and called the channel used by the Thrashathon's security guards. Frank told the guard who answered to put Joe Hardy on immediately, that it was an emergency.

That did the trick. Joe came on a few moments later.

"Joe—no time to explain! Get some skaters and head for the pros' parking lot! Hall's getting away in his truck!"

Frank switched the walkie-talkie to the channel the Bayport police used and quickly reached Con Riley. Frank told Con that Hall was fleeing the skateboard park, going west on Mainways Boulevard. Then he gave the lieutenant the car's license plate number. Con told him he'd send a car over immediately.

Seconds after Frank had returned the walkie-talkie to the attendant, Joe dashed through the parking lot with a group of skateboarders. Among them were Zack, Rick Torres, and the whole Zebra Boards team.

"You can't skate, Zack," Frank said. "You'll hurt yourself."

"I'm not going to miss out on this," Zack insisted.

"It's too dangerous," Joe said.

Zack must have realized that Frank and Joe were right, because he stepped off his board. "Okay, okay," he said. Then his face brightened. "I just got an idea." He raced back through the parking lot and disappeared.

Frank watched Zack for a moment, then turned to the crowd of skaters. "Hall's gone down Mainways Boulevard. We've got to catch him before he gets too far. I called the police, too, so they should be showing up soon."

"I hope so," Joe said. "If Hall's going fast, we'll never be able to track him." With that, he stepped on the skateboard and led the group out of the park and down Mainways.

Meanwhile, Frank knew there was no time for

145

him to get to the van. He turned to the parking lot attendant. "Hey, do you have a skateboard in there?"

"Yeah, I do. Some kid lost it here." He reached down and lifted up a battered board.

"Thanks," Frank said, grabbing the skateboard. "I'll return it later."

As he pushed off across the parking lot, Frank heard angry shouting ahead of him. He rode as fast as he could and quickly caught up with Joe and the other skaters. Hall's truck was rounding a corner.

"Come on, guys!" Frank called out from behind. "Don't let him get away!"

The group of skaters pressed on the speed. Frank lowered himself into a squat, taking advantage of a downhill stretch to pick up speed. He rounded the corner and saw they were closer now.

Joe and Rick were in the lead. Frank could tell they were only ten feet from Hall's truck. While he skated, Frank saw Joe pump his board and get an extra burst of speed. Before Frank could tell what his brother had planned, Joe had shot ahead on his board and grabbed the back of Hall's truck. He hung on and got a free ride for about half a block.

When Hall turned around to tell Joe to get lost, the truck slowed, and Joe grabbed the moment. He placed one hand on the side of the truck and brought both legs up in the air, the skateboard held on top of his sneakers with his free hand. He completed his move by flipping over and landing with a loud thud on the lid of the truck bed.

Rick caught the back of the truck and pulled the same maneuver. Frank pushed his board even faster and, finally, caught up with the Zebra team. They were almost at Hall's bumper now. Frank passed them and grabbed the back of Hall's truck.

Joe was banging on the rear window of the truck, trying to get Hall to stop. Rick was holding on to the passenger door and trying to open it to get inside. Just then, Hall slammed on the brakes.

Seeing that Hall was getting out of the truck and racing across the street, Frank skated after him. Before Hall could get very far, Frank had tackled him around the ankles.

"Let me go!" Hall yelled. "You can't pin anything on me."

"You're wrong, Mr. Hall," Frank said, holding Hall's arms behind his back. "We have enough evidence to put you—and your friend Danny Hayashi—in prison for a long, long time."

Frank dragged Hall to his feet. Joe and Rick came running over, and then the rest of the skaters came roaring up. Behind them was Zack, whizzing along on a pair of roller blades.

Zack snowplowed to a stop right in front of Hall.

"You're a rat, Chris Hall," Zack said.

Hall gave Zack a nasty look through narrowed eyes. "You're just lucky you have some resourceful friends, Zack. Otherwise I would have had that board a long time ago."

"Well, you didn't," Zack said. He turned to Frank and Joe and held out his hands for a high-five.

147

"Thanks, guys," Zack said with a grin. "Now that was some full-on thrashing!"

Frank glanced at his watch, which told him he'd been at the station for two hours, and wondered when Con would let them go.

"Are you paying attention, Frank?" Con Riley asked impatiently.

"Sorry, Con," Frank answered apologetically. "What were you saying?"

"I was just asking you and your brother how you figured out Hall and Hayashi were after Zack Michaels's skateboard."

"Well, Zack had told us Hall wanted to make a deal with him to manufacture his board design," Frank said. "But when I checked into Hall's company, I found out it was going broke."

"Chris was just pretending to want to sign a deal with me," Zack said. He had also been brought into Con's office, to complete the report.

"When Evan Hall told Frank that Chris was in serious financial trouble, that's when Frank started to put the whole thing together," Joe said, rubbing his eyes.

Con leaned back in his chair. "But what about Barb Myers?" he asked. "I thought you said that at one point you suspected her."

Frank nodded. "We did think she was after Zack's board. We found a paper cup with lipstick on it in the empty house across the street from Zack's. We thought she must have been spying on

148

Zack from there so she'd know when it was safer to sneak into Zack's workshop and sabotage his pool."

"She didn't actually do that to the pool," Con said. "Hall confessed to that, and to vandalizing Zack's workroom and turning on the gas in your house. Barb knew what was going on all along, though."

"Barb used to be Chris's girlfriend, so she thought Chris was going to let her in on the deal," Zack explained.

Frank gave Zack a curious look. "How'd you find that out?"

"Rick told me when we went back to the park after we caught Hall. Barb came clean about the whole thing after she heard that the police arrested Chris." Zack squirmed in his seat and moved his shoulder a bit. "I guess one cracked shoulder blade isn't so much compared to what could have happened."

"So she was the person in the house with Chris spying on you?" Joe asked.

Zack made a face. "I guess so. It's pretty hard to believe, though. We used to be friends."

"Myers has agreed to be a witness against Chris Hall," Con said. He crossed his arms on his desk. "She'll be a valuable witness, even if stealing the board wasn't her idea. Now then," Con went on, "the last thing we have to nail down is Danny Hayashi's motive for being the mystery skater, as you call him."

"Money," Frank suggested. "Scorpion Boards

was going to make a lot of money from Zack's design. Hayashi was also really jealous of Zack, so maybe that was also part of his motive."

"Have *you* talked to Hayashi about his motives?" Joe asked Con.

Con nodded. "When we told him we'd found the mystery skater's clothes in Hall's truck, he turned pale. Remember those missing sign-up sheets?" Con asked Frank. When Frank nodded, Con went on. "Danny stole them because he knew they would prove when he wasn't at the park. When Danny learned he was going to be charged as an accessory to attempted murder, he got really upset. Even though it was Hall who opened the gas on the stove in your house and did those other things, Danny knew about the plan. I think Danny might want to testify against Hall to get a more lenient sentence. Danny also admitted to going after Zack in L.A. with some of his friends."

"When Maggie finishes her exposé of this whole thing," Zack said, "Danny's never going to be able to skate again—no matter what happens to him."

"And Chris Hall won't be back in business, either," Frank added. "Maggie's going to do a full investigation of Hall and Scorpion Boards. She's waiting outside to interview us when we're done here."

"What about Rick?" Joe turned to Zack and asked. "Did you call Alpine Bikes?"

150

Zack grinned. "You bet. Right before we came here, I made the call. Rick can get his job back if he wants. And I told Mr. Travers about my skateboard design. He said he's interested in producing my board. He's been thinking about expanding his business into skateboards. Once he hears how radical my board performs at the Thrashathon, he'll be *dying* to make a deal.

"That was the plan I had that I couldn't tell you guys about," Zack explained to the Hardys. "I was hoping to give the design to Mr. Travers instead of Hall all along. I figured I owed it to Fred. But I didn't want word to get out to Hall, because I figured it wouldn't make him too happy. But first I had to prove that the board would perform."

"So that's what the big secret was," Joe said.

"And the other big secret is that Joe's now a first-class thrasher." Frank turned to his brother. "You know, Joe, you looked pretty good on that ramp today. Maybe you should turn pro."

"I was thinking about it," Joe said. "This Thrashathon is my first chance to make a good showing as a serious skateboarder. But it also might be my last."

"Why is that?" Zack asked.

"Well," said Joe slowly, "you may be out of the competition this year, Zack, but you'll be back."

"That's right," said Zack, laughing. "And if you skate against the Hawk next year, I'm going to make you look like a real amateur."

Frank laughed. "Maybe you should stick to detective work, Joe," he said.

"I think so," Zack said to Joe. "No matter how good you are at thrashing, when it comes to solving mysteries, you guys know how to make the most radical moves!"